BIBHUTIBHUSHAN BANDYOPADHYAY

stories

Translated from Bengali by
Rani Ray

Introduction
Tathagata Banerjee

THORNBIRD
NIYOGI BOOKS

Published by
NIYOGI BOOKS
Block D, Building No. 77,
Okhla Industrial Area, Phase-I,
New Delhi-110 020, INDIA
Tel: 91-11-26816301, 26818960
Email: niyogibooks@gmail.com
Website: www.niyogibooksindia.com

Design: Shashi Bhushan Prasad

ISBN: 978-93-86906-42-7
Publication: 2018

Printed at: Niyogi Offset Pvt. Ltd., New Delhi, India

Contents

INTRODUCTION

It is an unfortunate fact that the literatures of the Indian regional languages, or even the names of their great writers, remain relatively unknown outside their respective regions. Rabindranath is perhaps a special case, because his fame is of a special kind. Other Bengali writers like Bibhutibhushan, Jibanananda, Manik Bandyopadhyay etc., are well-known in Indian academic circles, but the average reader who does not read Bengali, knows little about them. The average Bengali readers, too, will not find it easy to name a best-selling Malayalam novelist or a great Gujarati poet.

One reason behind this is the non-availability of good translations. The Sahitya Akademi has done some work in this field, but it is too much for any one organization to translate the vast bodies of deserving literature in each regional language into 20-odd others.

A solution lies in attempts like this book. English is now not so much a 'foreign language', as it is a convenient platform for reaching out to a wide readership. Whether it can express Indian experiences adequately is a different question, but it is undoubtedly the most elegant solution. Verisimilitude depends largely on the translator's competence. On that count, Rani Ray has done a fine job.

Bibhutibhushan's world is populated by such a great variety of people and events, that it is quite difficult to describe exactly what he writes about, and to compile a 'representative volume'. He has love stories and stories about death, stories about the extremely rich and the dirt poor, about travel and stagnation. He has historical novels and bildungsromans, adventure tales for young people, and stories about illicit love for older readers. He has humorous stories and ghost stories, detective stories and stories about the afterworld. Narrators in his tales aren't always human beings—they may also be animals or departed souls. The setting of the action may be rural Bengal or the Kalahari desert, Beneras or Burma, a seedy lane in Calcutta's red light area or the haunted temples of Angkor Wat.

One thing that can be said to be common to most of his writings is his style of narration, the tone of his voice. Bibhutibhushan has a unique style of speaking—homely and laid-back. Listening to his voice, one thinks of things like an informal gathering of friends, lazy afternoons, rainy spells, story-telling sessions and hookahs. Even where the stories do not have a clear frame, it is often suggested by the tone of the narrative that the narrator is talking to an informal audience of close friends. With certain words, Bibhutibhushan habitually uses spellings which are closer to their actual homely pronunciation than to their common written forms. Many of these little things are, of course, lost in translation. But one can still appreciate the unorthodox way in which he often interrupts the telling of the tale by introducing unexpected lines like, 'My tale is now coming to an end', or 'At the time of my story, there still used to be horse-drawn trams in Calcutta', or the way in which his dialogues often drift off and digress from the main topic in an unliterary yet completely realistic way. These intensify the readers' feeling that they are sitting in a tight circle in a small dark room with the narrator, chewing idly on great brass bowlfuls of *muri* and sipping lazily on incessant cups of tea, while the narrator, perhaps hookah in hand, goes on with his tale in a slightly haphazard but peculiarly satisfying manner.

Yet, that delicate lack of organization is a conscious technique that Bibhutibhushan uses to build the atmosphere. Despite appearances, he is a very conscious artist who knows exactly what effect he wants to produce. The rambling, intimate style is the perfect frame for the kind of tale he tells, and is an important part of the meaning of his writings.

The stories in this volume are in no way representative of Bibhutibhushan. No selection or anthology can be representative of Bibhutibhushan, because there is too little that is 'typical' of him, and too much variety. However, there is a theme weaving in and out of most of these tales, discernible somewhere in plot and somewhere in character and lending them a semblance of unity, which, for lack of better expressions, can be called a theme of 'persistence', 'recalcitrance' or 'incorrigibility.'

Consider Krishnalal, the canvasser, who is a man of the city. The two foci of his life are the city and Golapi, who is a woman of bad repute. The crisis comes when his means of livelihood in the city is destroyed. He tries to accommodate himself in the country, where he owns some land and sources of sustenance, but soon finds that he cannot live there. The city is too much in his blood for him to find peace in his ancestral village. He has to return, and after a long period of strife, is restored to his previous profession and Golapi, through a reiteration of his old art of promoting medicinal ointments of a company for which he no longer works.

It has been suggested that the title 'Tiroler Bala', which is the Bengali name of the story translated here as 'The Bangle from Tirol', has a double meaning; the word 'bala' being an archaic synonym of 'woman'. The translator has done well to keep it simple, because that way it remains more faithful to Bibhutibhushan's apparently simple style of naming his stories. The narrative begins with the description of a train journey and two young people, a boy and a girl, who seem quite normal until we learn that the girl suffers from a kind of incurable insanity. The narrative interest here builds around the contrast between the girl's beautiful and peaceful appearance and the truth we are told about her. Barring a few oddities, her behavior is quite fetching, and we begin to hope that her brother had perhaps overstated the case. The illusion lasts till the horrible climax which leaves us in no doubt about the irredeemable depth of her madness.

There is the would-be author who cannot get out of his nineteenth-century style of writing, and keeps going back to the ancestral mansion of the girl he exploits, and the girl keeps taking him back because she cannot help loving him in spite of the things he steals from-her.

The story 'Ancestral Homestead', being about supernatural presences, is another example of Bibhutibhushan's deceptive nomenclature. The retired old man feels an urge to return to his ancestral homestead, but cannot stay there for very long. Like Krishnalal, he is a man of the city. A resident spirit manifests herself to him, urges him to stay on, to bring back the good old days of the household. She will not leave the place or show herself to anyone else. Each is frozen in his/her own world, touching the other but not being able to influence.

Whether this is a true thematic unity in these as well as the other inclusions, or merely an apology for one, the reader can judge for herself. But the enjoyment of what are, basically, eight fine tales sensitively translated, should be marred by neither theoretical considerations nor long introductions.

Let the telling begin, and the stories speak for themselves.

Tathagata Banerjee

Ancestral Homestead
Paitrik Bhita

The large, old-fashioned ancestral house stood high on the banks of the Madhumati river. Sitting in the veranda facing the river, Radhamohan tried in vain to read the book he held in his hand; his mind was not in it.

The little upcountry stream, the clumps of bamboo trees and the ancient mango grove coasting the opposite bank were absolutely charming; the neighboring garden had turned into a hoary forest. Radhamohan felt nice staying all by himself in the spacious building. It was so quiet—an ideal place to read or to write. The house had been home to his ancestors but no one had been living there for a very long time. Shyamakanto Chakraborty, Radhamohan's father, had moved out of the village during his adolescence. He had studied and earned plenty of money, staying at his uncle's house in Midnapur; he had also built a large house there. It was not that he never went back to his village, but his visits were few and far between. He never stopped long. A lawyer with a flourishing practice, he couldn't afford to drag out his stay. Radhamohan's distant cousins had been occupying the building all these years; now they too had taken off for somewhere else. It was impossible for anyone to make a living staying in a village. Radhamohan, however, knew that the bit of property he owned had to be looked after; the house could easily be reduced to rubble otherwise. Qualifying as a lawyer the year before, Radhamohan had taken over his father's practice. He had come alone to his village during the festive season to arrange for the sale and distribution of his estate.

His next-door neighbor, old Bhairab Banerjee, had been taking good care of him. Even though Radhamohan had arrived in the village with mind made up to cook for himself, old Bhairab had managed to coax him to go to his house for meals.

As Radhamohan sat musing, Kesto, Bhairab's eldest son, appeared on the scene.

'Dada, come for your tea…'

'Bring the tea here, Kesto. It's nice to be by the riverside during the evening…'

'Should I?'

'Yes, it's a good idea…now get along.'

Radhamohan hadn't any doubt in his mind that the village folk were very friendly towards him; they had behaved as if he were one of them. The old men were extremely sympathetic. 'O dear! You are our brother Shyamakanto's son! How can we allow you to get your fingers roasted cooking? Come home, dear, we are still alive.' Radhamohan felt grateful towards each and every member of the community.

Kesto sat and chatted with him while he drank tea. Then once again Radhamohan was alone. The night was dark but the starry skies had cast a radiant cover over the river. As he sat around, Radhamohan wondered why his grandfather had to build such a palatial house in this part of the world. His grandfather had been a police-inspector in those days. He must have made a packet but couldn't have been worldly-wise. Most people of his generation weren't. No one in his right mind would want to build a house, spending such a lot of money in a village overlaid with woods. What good was the building to Radhamohan now? Perhaps he would try and dispose the structure at the price of old bricks, if the people of the nearby brick factory showed some interest. All of a sudden, Radhamohan heard a gentle rattle and an exceedingly fair ten or eleven-year-old girl came and stood peeping from behind the door leading to the courtyard. The room where Radhamohan sat was lit up by a hurricane lamp. Some light from it had fallen on the veranda. Radhamohan was not sitting in the dark.

Old Bhairab would send either his son or his daughter to fetch him for his meals—he was *that* caring. Radhamohan gave a little chuckle.

'What is it, little girl? Has the rice been cooked already?'

The next moment the girl came out, looking rather diffident.

'What is your name?' Radhamohan asked.

'Lokkhi.'

'A nice name—can you read?'

'No.'

'Know how to sing?'

'No.'

'Well then—there's a problem. You'll have trouble in the marriage market. How about cooking?'

The girl nodded; she knew how to cook.

'Well…it's one qualification you have. What all can you cook?'

'Everything.'

'Everything? That's really great! Come and sit.'

The girl shook her head shyly. 'No, I can't stay.'

'Why not? Do you have work to do?'

'Not really…'

'Sit down for a while then.'

'No, I must be off now. You go for your dinner.'

'I will, but is the dinner ready?'

'Hungry, aren't you? Go—go and eat.'

The girl had already gone before Radhamohan could look back and say a few more words. He soon left for the Banerjee household for his meal.

Old Bhairab welcomed him warmly. 'Come in, dear boy—come in. Dinner is almost ready.'

'I know that—your girl had come to call me,' Radhamohan said.

Radhamohan was back at his house after dinner. He rather liked the solitude of the empty house, felt as if his revered ancestors were traipsing about the place unseen. His grandfather had played in this house as a child; his grandmother had placed her pink-white feet on its threshold as a newly-wed. But they had left the place and had put themselves up in a different country, forgetting where they belonged. Drowned in sleep, in the deep of night,

Radhamohan imagined his ancestors coming and standing in front of him, accusing him of desertion—'What harm have we done to you?' they were saying.

Radhamohan was up early next morning. He kept himself busy the whole day, but the little girl was back as he sat in the veranda in the evening, taking shelter behind the door. Radhamohan became aware of her presence only after a flick of a moment; the girl had slipped in so quietly—really shy, she was!

'O Khuki!'

'What is it?'

'Is dinner ready?'

'Dinner will be late tonight. They are preparing a meat dish for you.'

'Oh, really! There's to be a feast then, and all for my benefit! Oh, you don't know what is a feast is? It involves preparing sumptuous dishes. How would you like that?'

The girl smiled and remained silent. A nice girl, Radhamohan thought, doesn't say much, has a quiet modesty about her.

'Where's your *mamabaree*?' He asked.

'Can't remember…'

'Not remember? How's that possible? Don't you ever visit your maternal uncle's place?'

The girl shook her head. She didn't.

Radhamohan found the girl rather amusing but quite unabashed; there wasn't a hint of embarrassment about her.

This time the girl said, 'Why have you come alone?'

'Why do you think?' Radhamohan was laughing.

'Bring your wife and daughters along. This is such a big house, let them enjoy living here.'

'Would *you* like that, Khuki?'

'I would…very much. That's what I want.'

'Whatever for?'

'The house has lain silent for so long. There's no one to light the evening lamp.'

Radhamohan was taken aback. The little girl spoke out with such an adult voice—in the tone of an expert housewife!

'Does that make you unhappy?' he asked playfully.

'Bah! Doesn't it? You should all be here to blow the conchshell and light the evening lamp.' Then, rounding off her sentence she asked, anxiously, 'You must be very hungry, it is rather late.'

'Not at all, the night is still young.'

'But you are used to eating early…'

'How did you know that?'

There was no answer to that. Only an indistinct laughter rang in Radhamohan's ears. After some moments the girl said, swinging her head, 'I really like it—really like…'

'What is it you like?'

'That you are here. Nobody ever comes to this place… You can go. The meat must be cooked by now.'

'How do *you* know that the meat is ready?'

'But I do…go now.'

'Wait for me. I'll go and wash. We will go together.'

Washed and ready, Radhamohan couldn't find the girl when he got back. She was gone. Children are so restless, he thought to himself. But what a girl! Tittering like a fully-grown woman. Radhamohan laughed his heart out.

'Come in, dear boy, come in,' Bhairab Banerjee called out as soon as Radhamohan appeared at his door step. 'I was about to send for you. It has become rather late—we have added a meat dish to the menu. I told my folks. 'He can't live on dal and rice—just dal and rice. I'm lucky to have him with us for these few days—it's not that he can't afford…that's why…'

'What are you saying?' Radhamohan interrupted, embarrassed. 'Of course I'll eat whatever I'm served. I'm like your son. You can't treat me as a guest…'

The next evening Khuki turned up as usual.

'Come, little girl, I was thinking of you,' Radhamohan said.

'You…thinking of *me*?' The girl gave a loud laugh.

'Honest to God, I really was!'

'I know why,' the girl was grinning, joggling her neck like a child.

'So you do?'

'Yes, I know, but I won't tell you.'

Radhamohan had bought some sweets for Khuki. He had actually sent Amulya, Hari Nandi's servant to buy the sweets from Islamkati market—sandesh from Islamkati was famous in the locality. Amulya was nowhere to be found—no doubt he was out gossiping somewhere. Radhamohan felt rather irritated with him. He had wanted to make the girl happy with a gift of sweets; there was no hope of that now.

'No, you don't know why I was thinking of you. Tell me why.' Radhamohan didn't give up.

'I know.' The girl replied softly and gave such a worldly-wise smile that Radhamohan couldn't pursue the subject any further Her smile told him she knew his reasons. Trust Amulya, that village bumpkin, to keep a secret..!

'Come, give me the sweets,' the girl said, droll-like.

Radhamohan got up hurriedly to bring her the sweets but she was gone by the time he was back. The girl is so restless, Lord knew when she had left—what strange behavior! Radhamohan finally carried the sweets to the Banerjee household.

'Khuki is so shy—she simply ran away. I had this small gift for her.'

Old Bhairab laughed. 'Oh, so Khuki had gone to your place?'

'She comes everyday, sits and chats.'

'Is that so?'

'Yes, she's a bit shy—a child still.'

Khuki was again at her appointed place the following evening.

'Why did you go away so suddenly yesterday evening? I was really angry…' Radhamohan blurted out.

Khuki smiled and said nothing.

'Have you tasted the sweets?' he asked.

'Why…I savored it the moment you mentioned them.'

The next minute, her voice full of affection, she said, 'I am so happy you are here now. The evening lamp is lit, and the house no longer plunged in darkness. How can I feel nice if I am alone all the time?'

'Do you want to visit the town? Come, I'll take you along with me.'

'I want to remain here—what's there for me over there?'

'There are so many things—the talkies, all kinds of food!'

'So what? How do those concern me? Say you'll come here again.'

'I will, for sure. Why won't I?'

'But you didn't all this time. There was no one to light the evening lamp…I must go now. You're leaving on Tuesday, aren't you?'

Radhamohan was somewhat surprised. He wondered if by chance, he had revealed his travel plans to Banerjee. It must have been old Bhairab who had spread the news to the rest of the family.

Work took Radhamohan to another place for a couple of days and although he had returned to his village on the ferry late on Monday night, he didn't visit the Banerjees. Instead he went to sleep, eating some flattened rice he found at home.

Bhairab appeared early next morning as Radhamohan was getting ready to return to the city.

'Dear boy, how late was it when you got in last night? Where did you eat? You should have called us—you're like one of the family. Why are you so inhibited?'

'Could you ask your little girl to come here for a minute?'

'Of course, I'll call her at once. Stay a while.'

Moments later Bhairab returned holding a dark, eight-year-old girl by the hand.

'This is not she...must be her elder sister.' Radhamohan uttered.

'Her elder sister? But her didi is already married. She lives with her in-laws—you couldn't have met her.'

'Must have been some other girl belonging to your family then.'

'But there is no other girl in our family, dear boy. I wonder if it was someone else? No—there is no girl of that age in the locality. The village has only two Brahmin households. How old was she?'

Like a flash it came to Radhamohan's mind. 'She said her name was Lokkhi.'

'Lokkhi—who could she be? There's no girl by that name in the village. You must have made a mistake, dear boy, or you haven't heard right.'

'Possibly—I didn't get her name correctly—but who was she anyway? There's no mistaking I saw her!'

'Lord knows, I don't understand a bit of all this. But there is no girl by that name or that age in this village—of that I'm sure.'

Radhamohan took his leave of old Bhairab, mentally perturbed. It was such a strange affair. And why hadn't Khuki come to see him again?

Radhamohan went to Jabbalpur, the house of his paternal aunt, two years following his return from the village. Turning the leaves of an old family album, the photograph of a young girl caught his eye. He felt he had seen the girl before but couldn't recall either the place or the occasion. When he showed the photograph to his aunt, she exclaimed, 'How could you have seen her—she's my younger sister—your *choto pishi*. She died when she was twelve years old—you were not born then, your mother not even married. We stayed at our ancestral house in the village at that time.'

Pishima continued to talk as if to herself, 'Ah dear, I do remember vaguely now…she was quite good looking, that was forty years ago. Your father left the village and came away to Midnapur soon after that. We hardly went back. I had gone there only once, after my marriage—that must have been twenty years ago.

Holding on to the family album Radhamohan sat stunned. A moment later, thinking back, all of a sudden he asked, 'What was *Choto Pishima*'s name?'

'Lokkhi,' *Pishima* said.

The original Bengali story was first published in *Upalkhanda*, May 1945.

The Call

Ahoban

I was visiting my village during a vacation. With my ancestral homestead long since in a state of rack and ruin, I had no place to stay. My father's old friend, Chakotty, was mighty pleased to see me. 'At long last your thoughts have turned homeward!' he said.

I paid him obeisance, touching his feet.

'That'll do…may you live long son! Won't you build a house for yourself here?'

'But I earn precious little…' I demurred.

'What's all this talk about money, son? How much does a country boy need to live in his village? Come—build a roof over your head. I'll supply you with straw and bamboo. Come visiting from time to time. You are our own Naresh's son. To see you is happiness itself! Come and stay here—you may not find us alive for long.'

Then there were the others too who took hold of me.

'Put up at least a thatched hut,' they said.

I was feeling rather happy returning to my village after a long time. People I had seen as children had grown up beyond recognition; the young men I had known had become old.

I was walking towards the market place one day, taking the mango grove path, when I came across an old woman among the shadows of mango trees, with the looks of a worn-out Annapurna (The Provider), as depicted in the stories of the poet Bharatchandra—no mistaking that! She was hitting the ground with a stick she held in her right hand in a slow rhythmic motion. She was clutching a small string bag under her arm; I presumed she was heading for the market as well. I came to a stop. I am full of compassion when I see a woman mellowing with age like her. A unique sight indeed!

'Where are you off to?' I asked.

'To the market, dear boy—' She held her upturned palm across her eyes to gauge whether she knew me. Or perhaps because her eyes were weak. 'Who are you?' she asked, 'I don't think I know you...'

'You wouldn't...I am Naresh Banerji's son, I haven't visited for a very long time.'

'Maybe that's why...I never went about here and there in those days. I had no need to when he was alive. I had everything one could ask for: a granary full of rice, a cowshed surging with cows.'

'But I don't seem to know you, old woman!' I said.

'I can't mention his name dear—he sawed wood.' She turned her eager eyes towards me to see if there was flicker of recollection in mine. But there was no reason why I would remember someone who was a carpenter in the days of my childhood.

'Do you have a son?' I asked.

'I have no one dear boy, not a soul. There's the husband of my granddaughter, he doesn't give me anything to eat. My daughter died giving birth to the girl. I am in such bad times—I go hungry for days. I am off to the market now to buy three paise worth of salt. I managed to get hold of some rice earlier in the day.'

I took some paise out of my pocket and gave them to her. I thought I had settled the matter once and for all. Nothing like that happened. On the other hand, I embarked upon a strange experience centering around the woman—an experience I would have been hard put to believe had it not affected me personally.

Hardly was I up the next morning when I found the woman coming towards my courtyard, hitting the ground slowly with her stick. I was staying with an uncle belonging to my kin. He said, 'She's the wife of Jamir, the carpenter. He died years ago, when you were still a child.' The woman was already in the middle of the courtyard calling me.

'Where are you dear boy?'

I realized the woman couldn't see well at all—not surprising at her age!

'I am right here!' I proclaimed loudly.

'I was wondering who had given me money last evening and thought I must go to the Brahmin quarters and find out. I can't see well in the evenings.'

My uncle explained to the woman who I was. She sat under the shade of the jackfruit tree and babbled her head off. I gave her some more money before she left.

My holidays were already coming to an end. I left for Calcutta the following day, leaving money with my uncle to raise a small thatched cottage for me in the village.

I was in the village once again, in the month of Jaistha, to spend my summer vacation in the newly-erected thatched room. All this time, in my hectic schedule, I hadn't given a thought to the woman and wouldn't have—had she not turned up one day and sat facing me on the low platform in front of my room.

'How are you dear?' I asked.

'Is death willing to have me, dear boy?' She brought out some mangoes from the end of her torn saree and placed them before me.

'What are those mangoes for?'

The woman forced a smile with her toothless gums. 'O Gopal, my darling boy, I've brought them for you—mangoes from my own tree—really sweet. You must eat them.'

I was amused by her name for me. I didn't know why but I rather liked my new appellation. I had no one left in the village who could call me by that name. My mother and aunt had died when I was a child; there was no woman in the village old enough to call me 'Gopal'.

'Where do you have your meals, dear boy?' She asked.

'At my uncle's—'

'Do they look after you well?'

'They do.'

'Do you get enough milk to drink?'

'Khuti, the milkmaid, brings me some—not bad at all.'

'Khuti ! My goodness! Milk from her is a total disaster—more than half of it is water…I knew you didn't get enough to drink.'

The next day, hardly had the morning light shown itself, when the old woman was at my doorstep.

I scrambled out of bed, 'What brings you here so early? What do you have there?'

The woman placed her stick against the wall. 'See—I've brought you a jug of milk.'

'Where did you find milk so early?'

'The left-handed Hazra's wife calls me Ma. She has no one, she lives next door. I had told her last night, 'Daughter-in-law, my Gopal is not getting any milk, he drinks tea or something, milk the cow early, dear.' That's why hardly had the cock crowed when she woke me up saying, 'Ma, get up and take milk for your Gopal!"

'But why—why make all this fuss—it doesn't become you. Don't bring me anything, understand? How much should I give you for the milk?'

Perhaps the tone of my voice had turned rather harsh…I knew that no one in the village would touch milk belonging to a Muslim household. I was afraid someone, somewhere, might find out about it. I didn't want to get into any kind of scrape. My sudden rudeness made the woman slightly apprehensive; she asked fearfully. 'Why do you mention money, dear boy?'

'How can you get hold of milk without paying for it?' I said.

'But I told you—didn't I—that it's milk from my daughter's house?'

'No matter—you must take this money. She's also needy.'

Although the woman left accepting the money, from the way she talked I realised she had become utterly dejected. I felt a little sad. Did I do the right thing giving her money, I wondered. The woman had become so fond me, the milk had been her gift of love. Perhaps I shouldn't have behaved the way I did. However, I must add, that far from taking my rejection to heart, the woman barely gave it notice. She continued to appear at my place every morning without fail.

'O Gopal, see these are two tender cucumbers from my tree. Salt and eat them in front of me, dear.'

'Old woman, how do you manage?'

'The husband of my granddaughter ought to be taking care of me, but he doesn't always. Remember the woman I talked of? She's so good! She gets rice by husking other people's grains. She never eats without giving me a mouthful.'

'Do you live alone?'

'Yes—why not come and see how I live one day, O my dear Gopal! I had woven a cloth out of new date palm leaves for you to sit on, thought how could I make a Brahmin's son sit on our soiled mat? I said to myself 'Let me weave a new cloth and keep it ready so that my Gopal can sit on it when he comes.'

I couldn't visit the woman's house that time around, in spite of her intense wishing. There was always so much work, and on top of it there were incessant demands made by friends of my age. I was visiting the place after a long time, so naturally…But the woman never missed her morning visits during my days there. She would always bring me something—a ripe mango, a lemon, a bunch of raw bananas, or a slice of pumpkin—and I would occasionally give her two or four annas—one day a saree too. I noticed she never asked me for anything; on the contrary she never appeared empty-handed.

One day a few friends from Calcutta were there on a visit. I was sitting in the room having tea with them. I had prepared the tea all by myself inside the room as, according to the village clock, it was too early to light the kitchen stove. The woman arrived, hitting the ground with her stick. Standing outside, she called.

'Gopal, dear Gopal!'

I felt suddenly embarrassed. Why had she to appear when I was in the company of my Calcutta friends? Couldn't she have stayed away this once? The bother!

'Gopal dear…are you at home?'

'Yes, why do you ask?' I replied, slightly irritated.

'Just came to see my Gopal once…'

One of my friends asked, 'Who's she? Eh?'

'Someone from the village,' I said, trying to make short of it.

Another friend said, 'Is Gopal your nickname in the village?'

'Yes—no—maybe.'

'How hot it was last night,' the woman continued, 'I couldn't sleep a wink—were you able to sleep, dear boy?'

Good for you! I muttered to myself. What a nuisance early in the morning! Would the world have turned upside down if she hadn't turned up today? I was extremely annoyed.

My friend again asked, 'Who's she calling Gopal?'

'Err…it's me actually.' Giving a light laugh, I pointed a couple of fingers at my head. 'She's bit weak upstairs.' I added.

'I see…'

Trying to make things look normal and matching my words, I turned to the woman and behaved as if I were soothing someone completely off her head. 'Please go away now, I am very busy today…can't you see?'

The trick didn't work. The woman gave a hearty laugh.

'What do you think I have brought you today, Gopal? See this—'

Till then I wasn't aware the woman was hiding a dirty packet behind her back. She brought it out now and said, slowly opening it, 'The girl who calls me Ma was pounding rice. I said "What are you doing?" "This is flattened rice from the finest kind of rice grain, take some for your Gopal tomorrow, during the daytime," she replied. My heart was filled with joy—and she's here too—she wants to see you. She's such a poor, sad woman! Makes a living by flattening rice for others.'

And as if this wasn't enough, hardly had the oldie finished her speech when I saw a pale, middle-aged woman under the mango tree coming my way. More trouble was in store for me as I found my uncle also walking in my direction. This was really going to be the end of me, I thought. I had meals with my uncle; Lord help me if he came to know I ate food prepared by their hands. But how could I make him believe they were bringing me food for the first time when they were always bringing me something—milk today, flattened rice tomorrow. 'Go now—can't you see I'm busy?' I said gruffly. And—take all this away—bring them later. Go now!'

The woman looked somewhat surprised. 'But little rice…'

My uncle had almost descended on us by then; he was next to the boundary wall.

Gesticulating with my hands, I shouted vigorously at the woman. 'For heaven's sake, take these away, what a nuisance.'

Uncle said, 'What has she brought for you? What's old Jamir's wife saying to you?'

'Nothing of importance, she has something to sell—Come on, be gone!'

Lord knows the old woman hadn't come to sell anything or collect any money.

Uncle remarked, 'She seems to be a frequent visitor at your place.'

I turned the subject around. 'My friends are keen on angling. Could we go fishing at Bhaduri's pond, do you think?'

I came back to the village after an interval of five or six months, at the end of Ashwin. I had been there for some days when, sitting by myself in my room, I heard a woman calling out to me in a feeble voice, 'Babu, are you in?'

Coming out, I found she was the same person who had come accompanying the old one last Jaistha. Pulling the saree end tightly over her head, in shyness at my presence, she asked, 'When did you arrive, Babu?'

'About five or six days ago. Why do you ask?'

'So I heard…let me go and see him, I said to myself. That mother of mine sent me along saying, 'Go and see him.'

'Who?'

'The old woman, who used to come here. She's very ill—I don't think she'll last. She keeps pestering me everyday saying, 'When will Gopal come, when will he come.' I tell her, 'He has a job in Calcutta, how can he be here all the time?' How she loves you Babu,—you must have been her son in your last life—that's why she is so attached to you in this—please go and see her once—it will make her so happy!'

'Ah!' I said absentmindedly.

My mind was elsewhere; I was worried about other things. I had arrived in the village taking on the huge responsibility of canvassing for votes for two of my friends who were contesting in the municipal council election. I had to start out the next day—a car was at my disposal. I was thinking of how to go about it. I had no time to spare a thought for an old woman who might be ill somewhere.

'Will you come later in the day, Babu?' The woman asked.

'I'll see, I can't say for sure.'

'Please come, at least once, she may not live…'

I went to see the old woman when I started my rounds in the evening. A high-walled room with five layers of thatched roof caught my eye. I realized the woman's husband had been well off to have built such a spacious room when I was not even born. Everything indicated that. But there was no question that the room hadn't been repaired in a long time. Straws had fallen off the thatch, ropes dangled from the roof, and the mud plinth had cracked at places. The bamboo poles, which lent the room support, had become unstable.

The old woman was lying on a tattered mattress, her head resting on a grimy, soiled pillow. The adopted daughter of hers was by her side. 'O Ma, see who's here—see O Ma—' she spoke out. The old woman opened her eyes as soon as I went in. Recognizing me, she tried to get out of bed.

'Don't get up. What are you doing…' I said.

The woman was pleased as punch.

'Are you well, Gopal dear? Hey, give Gopal a place to sit, give him a place to sit…'

'I don't need to sit, it's alright, don't be so flustered!'

'Why are you bringing that—spread the date palm cloth for him.'

Then in the complaining tone of a mother or an aunt she continued, 'I had woven this cloth for you such a long time ago. It's become old and tattered now. You haven't come even once in all these days. I am so ill, yet you don't come even once to see me!'

'It's okay, lie quietly now, don't get so excited!'

A lot of people from the village had gathered seeing that I had come. Some said, 'She only talks about you—you, Babu. She has been longing to see you. We don't think she'll live much longer.' Tears were streaming down the old woman's faces.

'Gopal, please buy the cloth for the coffin, when I die,' she said. I asked my neighbor what she meant.

'Don't you know, Babu? A new cloth is bought to wrap around the body when a person dies.'

'Oh, I see.'

The old woman was really very happy I had come. She went on talking about so many things: What a brute of a person her granddaughter's husband was; how he hadn't bothered to look her up although she was so ill. As for the room—it hadn't been rethatched in 10 long years, the old thatch had rotted. She had mentioned it to her granddaughter's husband. He could only say, 'Build a small hut next to it and live there—I can't afford to put a covering on such an elephantine large room!'

'Tell me, son, how can I live like that? I, who am the wife of such a person! Fate is against me today, but does that mean I have to live in a hut?'

'What you're saying is correct,' I said, consoling her.

'Tell me how can that be.'

'Very true,' I nodded.

Today I can still remember the thatched room wrapped in the pale light of the evening; the old woman lying on her tattered mattress; the lean pumpkin tree under the eaves of the thatched building; the clumps of bamboo plants in the backyard and the bark of a stray dog in the neighborhood. Evening's quietness had descended and spread over the entire courtyard. Men and women were standing under the edges of the thatched roof, looking at the scene.

I gave the woman's adopted daughter money to buy fruit and medicine. I had the feeling the woman would not live long; she might never recover from her present illness. *But she did*—I was amazed to see how she pulled through. She came to see me a few times, leaning on her stick, before I left for Calcutta. She sat and spoke all kinds of gibberish to herself.

Two years passed by. The woman was always there whenever I was in the village, bringing me something or the other…but she had become very frail. The illness had robbed her of her former strength. She was never fully well again.

I said to her, 'Why must you come everyday—walking such distance?'

'See this ripe custard apple—I felt I must bring it for my Gopal.'

'Doesn't matter—you must not take such a lot of trouble to bring it to me.'

'But you won't ever come to visit me—will you?'

'I will—when I have the time—go home now.'

All of a sudden the old woman said, 'O Gopal, why aren't you married?'

'I can't find a girl, besides I am getting on in years…'

'Rubbish, you are not old at all—you are a young boy!' (I was forty years of age then).

'Well!'

'The Mukherjees have a grown up girl. She'll suit you fine. I will suggest the idea to them.'

'I'll send for you when I am in need of a matchmaker—go now!'

But she wouldn't listen. One day, Naru of the Mukherjee household came to see me. He said. 'Look here—I have something to say. The old wife of Jamir, the carpenter, came to our house and told the womenfolk, "Get your daughter married to Gopal." The women were puzzled. They had no idea who Gopal was. When at last they found out that it was you she meant, they were truly amazed. Have you said something of the kind to that oldie?'

I felt quite helpless and vulnerable.

'What are you saying?' I said. 'I haven't told her anything of the sort.'

'So you didn't? Well, I don't believe her, of course. But do caution the woman not to go about talking like that. It's a backward village, people might gossip.'

'Of course, believe me brother, I had no inkling about all this.' I gave the woman a good scolding the minute she appeared the next morning. 'Who has asked you to go and make such a racket. Has anyone begged you to become my matchmaker? There will be such talk in the village. This isn't a nice place. You better not come here anymore.'

The woman looked bewildered. 'Don't scold me, Gopal—don't. Find another girl if you don't want to marry that one. You don't care for Puti, do you?'

'All that rubbish again—' I shouted.

The woman was a simple, old-fashioned soul; she hadn't a clue what the fuss was about. In actual fact there were already rumors in the village connected with the matter. I became so angry with the woman that I stopped staying home in the mornings. I didn't want her to come and vex me anymore.

I had gotten up from an afternoon nap some 10 or 12 days later when I heard her voice. 'O dear Gopal!'

'What's the matter now—you here again!' I hollered.

'I've brought you a *batapi* dear.'

'I don't want any—go now.'

I had good reason to be angry, My uncle had ticked me off about the Mukherjee affair barely five days back.

❧

I didn't visit the village again for one long year—it could well be a year and a half. I went there again for a couple of days on my way back to Calcutta from Kashi, where I had been spending my autumn holidays. I had discovered I had a few free days left. I met Parshu Sardar's wife the minute I entered the village. She stood staring at me. 'O dear, so you've arrived today. The old woman died last night. She was calling for you again and again—that's what her adopted daughter told us.'

The woman's granddaughter's husband came to see me when he heard I was in town. 'You've come—help us to buy the cloth for the coffin; everything is so expensive these days.'

I recalled the woman saying, 'Son, buy the cloth for my coffin when I die.' I mused at how her loving soul must have beckoned me here from the faraway town of Baranasi. Perhaps deep down my heart I couldn't ignore her call.

I gave money for the cloth. Before he left, the grand daughter's husband said, 'You must come when we cover her with the earth—around noon.'

They were burying the woman under a colocynth swaying ancient Tittiraj tree among wild bushes, giving off the bitter smell of Sharat, the autumn month. I went and sat among the people—Abdul Sakur Mian, Namur Abedali, who I had studied with when I was a child, his son Gani—under the shade of the tree. Seeing me old Sakur Mian said, 'So you're here, Baba Thakur—come and sit with us. Care for a pull of the hubble-bubble? How did you manage to turn up the day the old woman is being laid in the earth? How did you come to know? She loved you so…Her spirit will be at rest getting your coffin cloth—come take a pull.'

They laid her on an old wooden frame of a cattle cart and covered her in a dirty *kantha* cloth. Two youths dug her grave. After she was put down everyone took their turn in throwing a spadeful of soil over her body. Sakur Mian said, 'You too spread some—her soul will rest in peace.'

I threw in a shovelful of earth and instantly felt her calling out 'O my Gopal,' like she did when she was alive.

The original Bengali story was first published in *Anandabazar Patrika*, Barshik Dalsankhya, 1937.

The Color of Mist

Kuashar Rang

The monsoon had arrived with a vengeance. It had been raining day and night without a pause. Sitting idly on his familiar chair in the boarding house, Protul became extremely irritated. How was he to go out? It was impossible to make for any place—anywhere at all, in the rain. Water was dripping from the leaking ceiling and seeping into the floor; he had been shifting his bedding from one corner of the room to another—how long could he go on like that? Rain began to pour even more heavily in the evening, making the atmosphere misty all around. The gas lamps bordering the streets flickered hazily through gaps in the moisture-laden smog. Protul lit up a bidi. He had exhausted a pack since the morning; there had been nothing for him to do but smoke. He had no money to buy cigarettes. Had he smoked cigarettes he would have consumed two packets of Cavender's Navy Cut by now. All of sudden, remembering he hadn't had his morning cup of tea, he got up to call the mess boy. Someone knocked at the door. It must be Harish, Protul thought. Had he remembered he hadn't served Protul his tea? Protul unfastened the door only to stare in surprise.

'There you are, Protul da, greetings. You are well, I hope! I have come to see you...'

A thirty or thirty-one-year-old man wearing a dirty panjabi and rubber slippers entered his room, carrying a small tin suitcase and accompanied by a nine or ten-year-old boy. Blobs of water ran down his umbrella, his wet shoes leaving damp marks on the threshold. A splash of rain had already found its way through the open door into the room.

'Come and sit down, Khoka. Go and touch your uncle's feet...stay—let me rub your feet dry. There! Now go!'

Protul still hadn't a clue about the person who had come to his lodgings in such foul weather. Did he belong to his village? Where else could he have met him? All of a sudden he remembered. It must be Sashadhar—Sashadhar Ganguli from Nathpur. But how could that young eighteen or nineteen-year-old lad lose his youthful good looks and become so old?

'Do you recognize me, Protul da?'

'Why, of course! Do come in. I'm seeing you after such a long time! How did you know I lived here? Are you okay? Who's the boy? Your son? How nice!'

Sashadhar gave him a wide grin, revealing a set of red-stained teeth. 'Won't I - tell me how long has it been since we last met? Come to think of it, 10 or 14 years at the least. I got your address from Jiban Bhattacharji, remember him? Jiban da was the secretary of our library.'

'But how could Jiban babu have my address? I haven't seen him for 12 or 13 years, not from the time I left Nathpur...'

'A friend of Jiban babu's brother-in-law happens to also be a friend of yours. You remember Radhika babu, don't you? Jiban babu got your address from him. You don't keep in touch hi! hi! But we keep ourselves posted about you! Ei Khoka, sit quietly. Could we have some tea, Dada? It is so chilly.'

The little boy immediately bawled out, 'I am hungry Baba, I'm hungry.'

The father gave him a snub. 'There you go again! Stop whining, will you? You had food only this afternoon.'

'Oh dear, why are you scolding him? He's only a child—of course he can get hungry. Just a minute, Khoka, I'll bring you something to eat.' After tea and snacks were consumed Protul said, 'So Sashadhar…what are you about?'

'I'm the Headpundit of Ramjibanpur U.P. School. What else am I good for? I had come to Calcutta for some work, taking a couple of days leave. By the way, will there be a place here for us to stay the night?'

'Why of course, you must stay. It won't be a problem. I will tell the mess people you're eating here tonight.'

Protul had gone to Nathpur some 12 or 13 years ago, taking a clerical job in the village municipality office. Nathpur Municipality was not that insignificant; about four or five villages came under its jurisdiction. People belonging to the district came to blows during election time. It had, besides, a library, a dispensary, a high school and even a police post.

A young eighteen or nineteen-year-old lad had come and greeted him when he was sitting by himself in his house one day. 'Have you come to our village recently, Sir?' He asked.

'Yes, do come in. What's your name?'

'Sashadhar. I have come to make your acquaintance. I see you sitting alone all the time.'

'That's nice; do sit down—do you go to school?'

Who was there to send him to one? Sashadhar published his antecedents on the spot. With his father dead, he had to shoulder all the family responsibilities, which included his mother, two sisters, three small brothers and, of course, a wife.

Protul was astonished. 'Do you mean to tell me you're married at this tender age?'

'Why, of course, I got married last year.'

But Protul was none too surprised at the mention of an early marriage of this undoubtedly handsome-looking fellow. Although the boy left after sitting with him for a while, he soon started to visit him regularly. Protul felt happy about it. He was new to the place and didn't know a soul. He was pleased the boy gave him company, was friendly. It took care of his free time. The two would meet in the evenings and chat for hours together.

One day Sashadhar came and invited him to dine at his place. Sashadhar's mother treated him like a son and fed him, showering him with motherly affection. Sashadhar's sister addressed him as 'Dada' the moment she saw him. Protul liked the way the family took care of him in that alien country. Soon Sashadhar began to arrive at his place to take him home the minute Protul was back from work. Protul too made a habit of having tea and snacks at his house. After a few days, however, Protul began to feel rather uncomfortable. Keeping in mind the family were not well-off, he could not accept their incurring so much expenditure on his account. He stopped visiting. It was the only step he was capable of taking; had he wanted he could have easily cooked up some excuse or the other for his absence.

One day Sashadhar turned up and said, 'You must come home today, Dada. Kana said she'll be mighty angry if I don't bring you home.'

'Kana?' Protul couldn't hide his surprise.

'Yes, Kana—my younger sister. Have you forgotten? Come, let's go now.'

Protul was at a loss, but he also felt rather happy. Kana was a fair-complexioned, comely, sixteen-year-old girl. She spoke charmingly, and was fairly well-educated for a village lass. How wonderful that she was showing some interest in him.

Kana stuck to Protul the whole evening that day. It seemed to him that his absence had deepened their liking for each other. Returning home, Protul thought Kana had become very dear to him. Why was that? He mulled over the matter in his lonely house. Kana was really nice, an intelligent and caring girl. She belonged to a family equal to his in caste and status. Oh! Was that why Shashadhar made such demands on him, pressed him continually to come home? Why Kana was excessively friendly, falling all over him? The idea assailed his mind almost immediately.

Once again Protul stopped going to their house. Sashadhar, however, remained persistent. He lost no time imploring Protul to visit. This time around, Protul couldn't be won over. He was suffering from an internal conflict: Was

Kana in love with him or was she merely trying to entice him into marrying her? Why was her mother showering him with affection, why was Sashadhar so eager to bring him home? Protul felt he was beginning to see the situation clearly at last. Kana belonged to a poor family that couldn't afford to procure a suitable groom for her. In that respect, Protul was covetable. He had a 30-rupee job, was young and attractive to look at. Everyone thought he was nice. Protul began to feel hostile towards Sashadhar's family, suspecting a deep selfish motive behind all their love and caring.

A couple of months passed by and August arrived, carrying the splendor of autumn. The sun dazzled for about a week, making the water reeds along the banks of the canal bloom. Mud and slush dried up. The Puja days were imminent. Protul sat and worried about his 10-day holiday when the municipal office would remain closed. It was on one of those very days he came to know the distressing news about Sashadhar's family from another person. Sashadhar's mother was on her deathbed. Sashadhar hadn't stopped visiting; he still continued to come for tea and gossip, but he didn't once mention his mother's illness. Why was that? Protul however couldn't remain indifferent; he went over to their house almost at once. Showing a lack of concern now was against his sense of courtesy and humanity.

Kana came and opened the door upon hearing him knock. Protul thought she was rather surprised to see him. 'How is Ma?' he asked.

'Come inside the house, Dada is not at home. He's gone to call the doctor. Ma isn't at all well!'

'Let me go and see her. I had no idea she's ill. Sashadhar hasn't been for a few days, but he hadn't said anything when he visited me some days back!'

'How could he—when Ma became ill only five or six days ago? Her condition worsened the night before last. She wasn't so bad earlier on.'

The first thing Protul noticed when he went in was the gloomy and unprepossessing aspect of their poverty. He, himself, didn't come from a rich family, yet here, there wasn't even a trace of the grace Protul's household had.

'Why haven't you come all this time? It seems you've forgotten us,' Kana said.

Protul was doubly aggrieved. Looking at Kana's tired, anxious face, her slightly mournful eyes, he felt he had been unnecessarily cruel in not visiting them all this time. Kana was such a good girl! In the time he remained at her place, Protul realised the girl's strong sense of duty, her steadfast devotion to her sick mother. Sorrow and distress hadn't paled her beauty. Protul had come across so many women in his life who looked nice when dressed up, but pretty unattractive if shabbily clothed, when their hair was not done up or when they just got up from bed. Kana's beauty was of the kind that didn't lose lustre no matter what the circumstances. She looked as fresh as a flower in blossom, as graceful and as pretty despite her erratic schedule, her sleepless nights, her anxieties and hard work. Protul was happy and surprised to discover this precious truth about her.

He started visiting Kana's house regularly to give her a helping hand in nursing her sick mother. He warmed water on the stove, moved her mother to one side of the bed to change the bed sheet, and he shelled pomegranate seeds. He tried his utmost to console the bereaved family when Kana's mother left for her heavenly home, in the early morning of the fifth day of his visit. He paid all the expenses involved in the cremation as Sashadhar was without a penny. He remained at the burning ghat till the end. On his return to Kana's house with the rest of the family, he stayed on to warm himself up and to clean his teeth by chewing neem leaves. Kana now gave him a lot of attention. She worried over his physical and mental health, his nights without sleep, served him tea at the right time, mixed oil and salt in a fistful of muri for him to eat. Kana didn't forget anything in her sorrow—Protul was very happy those days. He shelled out 20 rupees from his salary to Sashadhar a day before the *sraddh* ceremony (the funeral), telling him what he had to do. He prepared a list of invitees and ingredients for cooking. The funeral was to be a frugal affair; 20 Brahmins and about 20 relatives in all were to be fed on the twelfth day, the *niombhanga* day, at the end of ritualistic mourning. Protul had been discussing those details sitting in Kana's house when, at the end of their consultation, Sashadhar got up and left. Protul had to stay put. He hadn't had his tea, Kana would have been furious had he left without taking it.

Protul took the tea cup off Kana's hands as soon as she entered the room. 'Sit down, Kana,' he said. 'You must see to all the arrangements for tomorrow. Nabin Bhattacharji has prepared a list—take a look at it in the evening. Sashadhar has gone to do the shopping, see that no item is left out.'

'But…you've given the money?'

'What of it?'

'How much?'

'How does *that* matter—it's not a lot of money anyway. You may regard it as a loan. Sashadhar will—'

'Dada won't return a penny to you! It's all rubbish! I thought I should let you know that. And why will you spend so much on us? You've helped us out during Ma's illness; must you bear the funeral expenses as well? As if you have stashed away a fortune in the bank! All you have is a 30-rupee job. What will you give to your family—your father, mother, brothers and sisters? How will you cope with the cost of living? Dada is sitting at home, unemployed. He won't ever pay you back—that's his temperament. I am telling you not to give him a penny. How does it matter if the funeral ceremony can't be held? Why must you dole out money?'

Protul stared at Kana in amazement. He felt, all the more, that the girl was the epitome of commanding innocence. Her large eyes betrayed a blunt candour as yet unschooled in pretense or flattery. Kana was speaking to him with a new voice. Protul was astonished to no end. He felt he was regarding her in a way he hadn't earlier. His heart was filled with admiration. Kana was no ordinary girl!

With the funeral ceremonies over, Protul continued his regular visits to the family. He had gotten used to Kana's ministrations, and couldn't detect even the slightest negligence in the care and attention she gave him. Recovering from mourning, Kana was even more lovely to look at; her body glowed with the magnetism of youth.

He resolved in his mind to broach the subject without delay—but how was he to go about it? There was nothing stopping them from getting married at the end of the period of mourning, they could get engaged in the meantime. It didn't look nice mixing freely with a girl outside the family without some firm commitment on his side; He went to her place in the afternoon.

Kana was delighted. 'There you are Protul da, turning up just as I was about to announce you'd be here any minute. There's no milk for tea. Piltu left the pan uncovered and the cat has lapped it all up.'

'Come and sit beside me, Kana, there's plenty of time for tea.' Protul knew Kana had taken on the role of a mother to her siblings in the absence of their own. She had become the mistress of the house now. He also saw how the little custodian of the family often found herself in a tight spot for lack of funds. Kana, however, never told him anything, ever, but he guessed that was the case, like he did on that particular day.

As Kana went out Protul asked her little brother, Binu, 'What have you eaten, little boy?'

'Rice.'

'Have you had something to eat now?'

'There was nothing to eat, not even rice...Didi hasn't eaten anything.'

He asked Piltu, Kana's eleven-year-old sister when she came in, 'Why hasn't Kana eaten?'

'There wasn't any rice. Didi borrowed some from the Sarkar's earlier in the day. Dada left for somewhere yesterday, he hasn't gotten back even now. Mahesh Chakotti refuses to supply us with groceries because we owe him money. What will Didi do now? To whom can she go?'

Protul thought deeply about all aspects of the situation. Kana was unable to manage household expenses; if he were to help her out with some money now it would seem as if he were giving her alms. For Kana to accept his philanthropy would mean compromising her self-respect. Protul wouldn't dream of putting her to shame, yet how long could Kana continue her life in abject poverty? Considering all things, the marriage proposal could not wait. He decided to settle the matter with Kana on that very day. He would tell Sashadhar about it later. Sashadhar lacked the qualities of a real man—it hadn't taken Protul long to find that out.

Kana came in with the tea. 'It's gotten a bit late, Protul da. There wasn't a drop of milk in the house. I have brought some from my uncle's. See if the tea is okay'

'Why are you running around in a state of frenzy? Come and sit down, I have something to say.'

It was winter evening. The *banamouri* shrubs in the woods surrounding Kana's little house had started to flower. A strong aroma had filled the air of the winter afternoon. The red rays of the declining sun falling on Kana's dilapidated ancestral lodging intensified the antiquity of the building. Kana looked up at Protul with eager eyes. 'What is it, Protul da?'

'I have to tell you something—you mustn't take it amiss—I have been thinking it over for the last several days but couldn't bring myself to talk to you. Will you marry me, Kana? I would consider myself very fortunate if you…'

Kana was silent. No one spoke for some moments. Then in a subdued voice Kana slowly said, 'That's not possible, Protul da!' Protul was struck by surprise. He little expected her reply.

'Why not?' he asked.

Fixing her gaze on the floor, Kana faintly continued. 'No, no, that can never be, Protul da. There's a reason, of course, but I can't talk about it now. We can't get married, that's all.'

Why couldn't they marry? Was she in love with someone else? But he hadn't seen any young man visiting the family. What could be the reason then?

'Is the obstacle in the way of our marriage hard to overcome? I want to know why you can't marry me.

'It's difficult.'

'Won't you tell me why it's difficult?'

'But don't you know…Hasn't Dada told you anything?'

Protul's astonishment increased by volumes. What was it that he was obliged to know? What was it that Sashadhar hadn't divulged?

'No, Kana, I don't understand a thing about what you're saying. What could have Sashadhar told me?'

'I'm a widow.'

'You…?'

'Yes! I was married when I was eight years old. I became a widow when I was thirteen years of age. It's five years to date.'

Kana…a widow? Protul's head was spinning madly. He felt faint. What an irony of fate! He had been weaving such incredibly romantic dreams around the girl, had wrongly accused her family, in his thoughts, of having designs on him. His heart was suffused with feelings of guilt and shame.

'But, Kana, I didn't know anything about this. No one had told me!'

'But I thought you knew…that Dada had told you about me. I'm struck by your ignorance.'

'Can I say something…a lot of widows remarry in our society these days.'

'Leave such thoughts…what cannot be, won't be—what's the use of raising the issue?'

'But I won't give in. Why won't you marry me, Kana, answer me to my face…I am interested in seeing you happy, I can rebuff society and all its norms for that.'

Tears welled up in Kana's eyes, they streamed down her cheeks. Wiping the tears with the free end of her saree, she said, 'I beg of you, Protul da…'

Protul didn't add another word. The next day he handed his resignation letter to his office, giving them a month's notice. He decided there wasn't any point in his staying on; he wouldn't stay in Nathpur any longer.

Protul didn't mention his resignation letter to anyone in Kana's household, not during his daily visits the following month. When he went to see them for one last time before leaving, he said, after a casual conversation, 'Kana, I'm leaving this place for good, tomorrow.'

'You're going away…but why?' Kana looked at him in surprise.

'I've left my job.'

'What are you saying…'

'That I have given up my job…I'm leaving tomorrow.'

'Are you telling the truth?'

'Why should I lie?'

'But you haven't mentioned anything like this earlier!'

'No, I hadn't and what is the use? I know I'll be going away.

'Why? Has life here become intolerable for you? Have you found a better job elsewhere?'

'Not at all.'

Kana remained silent, Protul joined in her silence.

After some time Kana said, 'I knew you would leave—sooner or later—you don't belong here. How could we bind you to this place…and why would you listen to us.'

'I have caused you so much misery, Kana, do forgive me.'

Kana kept quiet and their conversation ended on that note. Protul left by train the following afternoon. He had thought of visiting her one last time but couldn't make it.

Protul thought of Kana right through the journey. Poverty and deprivation was her lot in life. She was a young widow of a poor family, had no one but an elder brother to look up to. Her life was dark. There's wasn't a ray of hope coming from any direction. Protul felt a tug at his heart. What was he abandoning Kana to?

The next minute, however, he recanted. 'The bother,' he said to himself. Kana was among her own family, living in her parental home. She had an elder brother. What was she to him, anyway?

Protul got married six months later in the month of Phalgun, giving in to his mother's pleas. His father-in-law was the owner of two or three coal mines. The mines were in a bad shape. Goods were getting stolen, and business was suffering due to the absence of efficient, responsible management. Protul's father-in-law offered him a place in his establishment. Protul ought to look after the mines instead of working for an outsider. He would be drawing the same pay. The arrangement would not only benefit both of them, there was every chance Protul would improve his fortune. Protul agreed to the proposal, the mines began to flourish under his competent supervision, and in a couple of years he was able to turn the situation round.

Protul set himself up in Buddchawk, in a furnished bungalow three miles down the Asansol railway station, with his wife and son. He had had a son in the meanwhile. He lived in style—had to for the sake of his job. But Kana's memory continued to haunt him—he knew not why. He had a beautiful, well-furnished bungalow, money and happiness; Kana had no share in all this. She was amidst unredeemed poverty, stuck in the old, broken down, brick-built house. His heart twinged in pain. He realised she occupied the core of his being and that there was no forgetting her! Protul's wife was the daughter of a rich man. She had enjoyed all the comforts of life since she was a child. What was the point in caring for her, fulfilling her needs, buying her new gifts? It was like carrying coal to Newcastle! If only he could do something for Kana, who was denied of everything in life... if only! Why was life so unfair? The person who enjoyed all creature comforts continued to enjoy them whereas the person who didn't, remained a destitute forever. Why was it he couldn't make that person happy, look after her needs, take care of her? Why was life like that?

Those incidents took place some four or five years ago. Protul was in Calcutta for some days now, looking for a job. The mines were still there but Protul was without a wife. He was back to square one. There was a history behind it. Briefly, Protul hadn't been happy staying at his father-in-law's after his wife's death, a year ago. He suspected his father-in-law was also not pleased about the arrangement. Protul had come away to Calcutta with his son and had put himself up in his familiar boarding house. He was looking around for a job, when Sashadhar turned up unexpectedly, as if from nowhere. It was strange! Making him happy with a hot cup of tea Protul asked, 'What brings you here? Are you keeping well?'

'I am okay. Heard from Jiban da you were staying here. I believe you are hunting for a job. That's why I've come. I've heard everything about you.'

'What's the problem? Is there a job in the offing?

'Yes, the same clerical job in the municipal office is lying vacant. They will take you in immediately. Kishori Chatterji is the chairman now. He had liked you a lot, besides he's one of us. Come, put in an application straightaway. You can go for your interview after I write back to you.'

Nathpur! Once again? And a 30-rupee-month job. Incredible! So be it! Protul handed in his application to

Sashadhar the very next day. He needed a job; 30 rupees a month was enough to see himself and his son through. His parents were still alive but they didn't depend on his earnings.

After a fortnight, Sashadhar wrote asking him to come and meet the chairman. The job had been fixed. Protul travelled to Nathpur with his son. He hadn't visited the place in 10 years, yet he felt he had left the village only yesterday! He didn't ask Sashadhar about Kana, felt hesitant about it—he didn't know why. Though unsuccessful in raising the topic, Kana came to his mind the minute he got off the train. He would live the rest of his life in the place where she lived, he resolved.

❧

It was almost one in the afternoon when he reached Nathpur station. Sashadhar was waiting for him.

'Protul da, I've rented the same old house for you…there won't be a problem. Kana has asked you to come home for a meal. The job is secure; everything has been taken care of.'

'I don't have to eat now, Why not take Khoka along with you. I'll join you after work. We fed ourselves before boarding the train.' Protul went over to Sashadhar's in the afternoon, having met the chairman. Kana came and touched his feet.

'Protul da, so—you've remembered us…after all this time?'

Protul stared at her in amazement. Where was the girl he knew—that exquisitely attractive young woman? He could hardly recognize the person who stood in front of him. Kana had become considerably thinner. Her youthful good looks had all but faded away, although she was only twenty-eight years old. Protul eagerly scrutinized her face in the hope of discovering some traces of her earlier beauty. He couldn't find any. Almost at once the feelings he had had for her vanished into thin air. Kana seemed like another woman, not the girl he had once known and loved; she couldn't evoke any emotions.

Kana, however didn't stint giving him attention. She served him betel leaf after the meal, 'You haven't been here for such a long time, Protul da, I've so much to tell you. Stay back for a while, please.' Protul kept thinking how lucky he was for not keeping in touch with her, for not marrying her. He had made a fortunate escape from life's distressing realities. God had saved him!

Coming out of the house along with his son after an exchange of the usual pleasantries, he heaved a sigh of relief. He called Sashadhar early the next day. He said, 'Brother, my son has been ill since last night—your country is infested with the malaria bug. I can't take up a job here, I must look for one elsewhere.'

The original Bengali story was first published in Prabashi, October-November, 1940.

THE PHOOLBAREE OF BENIGI

Benigir Phoolbaree

I would meet Lalit babu every evening at Kastaharini ghat in the town of Monghyr. I was holidaying at my *pishima's*. It was my first visit to a town to the west of Bengal; I had had no previous experience of living in those regions. As I was getting ready to set out for the place, I recalled a friend saying, 'Your shoes won't need a coat of polish there…you'll see!'

It didn't take me long to discover how close he was to the truth! The shoes got so thoroughly plastered with a russet-colored dust, within 15 minutes of going on the road, that any enthusiasm I might have had for shining my shoes to a gleaming finish dwindled in no time. There was dust everywhere in town and out of the place—wherever I was obliged to go. Gradually, I felt less and less inclined to stir. It was then that I discovered the banks of the River Ganges as the most suitable place for taking a stroll. I would roam the town and finally settle down for the night, alone, on the steps of Kastaharini ghat.

One day a middle-aged gentleman came and sat beside me. We became friendly talking. I came to know his name was Lalitmohan Ghoshal, that he hailed from the Hooghly district and had been footloose for the greater part of his life. Stricken by malaria fever, he had come to these regions from Bardhaman town, where he had been living, some 10 or 12 years ago. Soon we were seeing each other every evening, exchanging camraderies late into night.

One day Lalit babu said, 'You haven't told me you are a writer!'

'Where did you learn that?'

'Why…everyone is talking about it. I heard you had given a lecture in the Bethune Bazar library. My landlord's son was among the audience.'

'Well…that's likely.'

'I am so happy to have met you, Sir. I have also tried my hand at writing at one time, you see. I have great respect for literary people like you. I hold you in high esteem although you are so many years my junior!'

'Rubbish!' I said, giving him a befittingly modest smile.

'How I would love to show you my literary pieces. Hi! hi! I had quite a reputation as a writer at one time. My novels had run into two or three editions. Do come to my humble lodgings one day.'

I was somewhat surprised to hear what Lalit babu said. There wasn't a single work of fiction, worth the name, I hadn't read as a young boy. I had never come across a novelist bearing the name of Lalit Ghoshal. I had no memory of the existence of such a person.

One day, out of sheer curiosity, I accompanied Lalit babu to his house. He lived in a single room in the exterior part of a small building beside the railway track. The room was a mess; it looked as if it hadn't been swept or dusted in years. The bedding was even grimier, with cotton wool spilling out of split, bare pillows. One look at the filthy clothes he wore at home told me Lalit babu's circumstances could not be happy. Lalit babu, however, welcomed me warmly to his house. 'Have some tea, please, since you have deigned to visit me.' His hospitality left no stone unturned. He gave me tea prepared by his own hands and a couple of homemade bread pieces smeared with molasses. He brought me a steaming hubble-bubble and was disappointed I didn't go in for such things. Having had his fill of tobacco, Lalit babu unfolded an old, bound exercise book, then looking at me, smiling shyly, he said. 'See this—I would like you to have a look at the reviews of my work which were published in the papers.' I began to read the exercise book with great interest.

Reviews of Lalit babu's novels, published some 25 years ago, in 1910 or 1912, in the leading newspapers and magazines, like *Bangabasi, Englishman, Hitabadi, Bharatmahila* etc., were cut out and pasted on the leaves of the book. Every piece of paper bore the name and date of publication, written in his own hand in black ink. The bits of paper had turned brittle and yellow, although the book was not sooty. I realised Lalit babu had been taking good care of it, dusting the book regularly.

As Lalit babu began to read out the reviews, one by one, I realised that his work had been well-received at one time. Lalit babu's face and eyes were glowing with joy and pride; he looked utterly transformed as he went on reading.

One reviewer had compared him to Bankim Chandra; the review had appeared in an English paper, edited by an Englishman. I had no doubt at all that the English had as much understanding of Bankim's genius as they had of Lalit Ghoshal's literary merits. I was getting ready to leave when Lalit babu said, 'I have two books lying ready with me for a long time. You live in Calcutta and must be knowing all the publishers…could you please do something about them?' He insisted I carried the two fat and heavy exercise books home.

Lalit babu had repeatedly asked me to give his manuscripts meticulous attention, but the moment I finished perusing the two volumes I began to feel sorry for the man. Lalit babu wrote in such an old-fashioned way, in a cramped and cumbersome style. Sentences stood out stiffly like wooden dolls. Moreover the stories ended with an explicit moral message: a just distribution of desserts, rewarding the good, punishing the guilty. I knew that they would never go down with modern readers, but couldn't bring myself to tell him that. When we met again at Kastaharini ghat, he asked, 'Have you had a good read? What did you think about them?'

'They are wonderful—no one writes like that these days.'

There was some truth in what I said.

Lalit babu was absolutely delighted. 'Hi! hi! hi! you are a writer—you know what's what—I don't have to explain anything to you. People write so differently nowadays—they don't know how to use the language! Just think of the great writers of the past: Bankim, Hembabu, Nabin Sen and others. People only talk of Robi Thakur now—Robi Thakur, ughh!' Lalit babu turned his face away in disgust and dismissed the subject. I nodded my head in approval, little realizing I hadn't been very circumspect in praising Lalit babu's work. He wouldn't let me be in peace, but pestered me day and night to do something about his manuscripts. I was very soon compelled to forgo the pleasure of my evening promenade by the Kastaharini ghat.

I hadn't laid my eyes on Lalit babu in five or six days when my servant came in and said, 'A woman is looking for you, she is standing outside.'

I was struck by surprise. A woman looking for me—who could she be? Coming out of my house I found a good-looking young girl standing shyly under the papaya tree in the front courtyard.

'Who are you?' I asked

Her head hung low, the girl spoke out in the local Hindustani dialect. 'Lalit babu wants you to see him soon, Babuji.'

'Lalit babu? Why, of course, I will go to him later in the day.'

As she left, I wondered who she was. Was she Lalit babu's maidservant? But how could that be? I had never seen her there. The girl was certainly good-looking, well-built like the women of that country. She was exceedingly fair-complexioned and had a lovely expression on her face.

I went over to Lalit babu's house that very evening. He was warming water for tea in a pan, adding milk and molasses. He gave me some to drink.

'A woman had come to call me,' I said. 'I have been rather busy for some days, I couldn't find the time...'

'Oh, so Monia had gone over? I am so happy you've come. I was wondering why you hadn't visited.'

After a brief prelude, Lalit babu brought up the subject of his books all over again.

'Know what—I am a bit short of funds. It would be really nice if you could push the books in the market. The money would come handy. That's why I had given Monia your address. Have you made any progress in that direction?'

I realised 1 was in deep trouble! I had no idea what I would do with the books and little knew the reason for my reluctance to tell Lalit babu the truth. Instead, I informed him that I had written to a couple of publishers, and that I hadn't heard from them as yet. I would let him know when I did.

'You needn't take the trouble of coming over here again. Monia knows your place now. She'll go and find out from you in a couple of days.'

'Does Monia work for you?' I asked.

Lalit babu gulped and stammered. 'Yes...you mean Monia, I suppose.'

Monia turned up at my house the following third day. By then my curiosity had got the better of me. 'How long have you been with Lalit babu?' I asked her.

Monia was not given to conversation; I could hardly hear what she mumbled, her head bent. I gave her five rupees. 'Tell Lalit babu Calcutta has sent the money.' I said.

Lalit babu went on harassing me for days after Monia's visit. He wanted to know which publisher was showing interest in his manuscripts and what we were corresponding about. The books were, in the meanwhile, lying near-forgotten in my room. The Calcutta publishers were not a pack of fools to give money in advance for the likes of those manuscripts. Openly, I said, 'They were not sure they wanted the books; they have given the money in case they decide to have them!'

Lalit babu was happy about money coming his way during his hard days; he had neither the time nor the inclination to find out who had sent the money and why. I kept sending him a few rupees through Monia, who turned up at my place, on a regular basis, every week. I had begun to feel really sorry for Lalit babu. He was a middle-aged, handsome-looking man, and a writer to boot. There was no doubt in my mind that he had fallen on evil days, and that he hadn't a soul or a distant relative around who could take care of him in this remote alien countryside. At times he did ask for the name of the publisher who was sending him money. I cooked up names of fictitious publishers, made up stories about imaginary correspondence, and more often than not, changed the subject and talked about other things.

I left Monghyr at the end of that winter. I went over to Lalit babu's place before I came away. 'Sir, what happened?' he asked.

'Everything has gone wrong. The publishers have folded up their business. The brothers who owned the firm have come to blows. There's a court case going on. Under the circumstances they couldn't…That's why they have sent the manuscripts back to me the day before yesterday.'

*Fate conspired to take me back to Monghyr after a lapse of three years. Lalit babu came to my mind as soon as I arrived. I didn't find him at Kastaharini ghat and asked around. No one could tell me whether he was still there or had left. One day, hiring a light horse carriage, I ventured out of town. I noticed a big country house when I was six or seven miles up the country. I asked the tom-tom-wallah whose house it was. The man spoke fluent Bengali; he said, 'This the Benigi *phoolbari*.' I was immediately seized by a longing to see the place.

'Will they take us in?'

'Of course, a Bengali babu lives here, why won't he?'

The mention of the Bengali babu increased my desire to visit. I walked into the garden, keeping the driver and carriage posted at the gate. The garden was a strange sight indeed! I saw at once that what had been a large and luxurious country house was now in a state of utter ruin. Nevertheless, I fell captive to the charm of the abandoned villa surrounded by wild woods.

The graceless, dilapidated house with peeling plasters, stood where a gravel-spread road threaded its way beyond a cluster of bushes. Huge, ancient trees: the oak, fig trees, neem and mahogany trees, the flowery gulmohar and trees that had digitate leaves grew wild everywhere. A thick undergrowth of fern and thorny shrubs, interlaced with wild brambly rose plants, ran like a carpet on the ground. An elephant trunk carved out of black stone, drain pipes with goat heads as spouts, a wrought-iron garden bench with a broken arm, and a flacky terrace constructed out of tightly-knitted stones came into my sight. The light panicky movement of the squirrel in the underwood, the call of the wood pigeon, sunshine peeping through the gaps in the thick growth, knots of chameli blossom next to a waterless fountain, the sweet scent of flowers, the incessant cooings of a *dahuk* bird perched on an ancient oak tree, and the crackly sound of a chameleon darting to and fro among slim, dried-up reeds—all had combined to create an atmosphere of deep repose.

I realised that the place, which had once been a rich man's pleasure garden, had now fallen to disuse due to depletion of wealth. I stood beside the stone fountain and regarded the scene of decay. I thought I should write a serious piece on the subject of the transience of wealth. Really, what was the point in churning out mindless, light-hearted stories when one could, as well, compose something that might do good to man and society? All of a sudden I came to my senses with a start. I saw Lalit babu, the gentleman from Kastaharini ghat, coming towards me down the gravel-threaded path.

'Why, it's Lalit babu, how come you are here? Do you remember me?' I asked. Remember he did, and was exceedingly pleased as well. He talked me into accompanying him to the old house.

'You must stay on…there's no problem at all. I'm meeting you after such a long time! I have so many things to tell you.'

We went and sat on the stone bench in the large courtyard of the ancient building.

'So, what's all the news? I arrived a fortnight ago and have been looking for you everywhere. How did you land up in this godforsaken place? Have you bought the property? Who else is there?' I shot off a volley of questions.

Lalit babu simply laughed. 'Don't get so flustered,' he said. 'You'll get to know everything in good time. Let's have some tea in the meanwhile. I'll send for some…'

I hadn't guessed who Lalit babu had given his orders to, but half an hour later a bashful-looking, beautiful Hindustani girl came and placed tea and fried papads in front of us. I immediately knew her.

'Do you recognize her?' Lalit babu asked.

'I do, of course! She's Monia. So she works for you still?'

Lalit babu smiled at my words; an embarrassed smile also gave way on Monia's face. She looked the other way. I couldn't imagine what I had said to amuse both of them.

'Monia, go and get us some more tea,' Lalit babu ordered. After she left, he said 'It's difficult to say who works for whom! You never got to know Monia—did you? This house actually belongs to her. It was her father's place. It is she who has given me shelter.'

I was really astonished now. I had always regarded Monia as Lalit babu's maidservant. Never in my dreams had I imagined she was a princess in disguise!

'But she used to work for you while you were in Monghyr,' I protested.

Lalit babu was all smiles. 'Did you ever see her working in my place? You had thought that up because she went to call you. You didn't know it for a fact.'

'What is the truth then, do tell me. Where lies the mystery?'

'Monia's mother was not married. She was the daughter of a poor Brahmin family man from Mujjafarpur district. Monia's father was a rich landlord. He had brought both the mother and daughter over here when Monia was still a child. Now that both her parents are dead, Monia is the sole heir to the property. It's as simple as that!'

'Not simple at all! How did you get to know Monia? Why do you stay here? Who are her guardians? I can't say these are simple matters!'

'Those facts are also straightforward. I had worked as a private secretary to Monia's father. I became her guardian after his death. There was one other, a lawyer from Monghyr by the name of Kamaleshwari Sahay. He conspired with others and threw me out. That was why I had to stay in Monghyr town for one whole year. Monia would often go there to see me and I would send her to you to collect money. She has herself helped me out in so many ways.'

'Is she unmarried?' I asked.

After a moment's silence Lalit babu continued. 'Who would want to marry her knowing her family history! You know what this country is like.'

The sun in the meantime had reclined to the west, and the day was beginning to run out. Sitting on the stone bench beside the chameli bush, Lalit babu and I became engrossed in conversation.

Monia appeared again with tea.

'Can you recollect this gentleman?' Lalit babu asked her.

Monia nodded, smiling.

'Where do you think you've seen him?'

'In Monghyr, at his house.'

Then she turned to me with a grin on her face, and spoke out in her familiar local Hindustani dialect, 'Have you been keeping well, Babuji?'

'Yes, and you, Monia?'

'You must stay back the night,' Lalit babu insisted. 'I don't have anyone to talk to in this place. You simply must—now that you are here—Monia do ask him…'

'I have already asked—do stay back Babuji. I'll be so happy if you do!' Thereafter I had no option but to stay on.

I found Monia genuinely pleased I stayed. 'What would you like for dinner?' she asked. 'He eats puris, will the same do for you?' I had a good look at Monia. She was really a beautiful girl with the physique of a Hindustani woman and the comely facial expression of a Bengali girl. A wonderful mélange of appeals. She had a pinkish complexion like one finds among Kashmiri women, a head full of thick black hair and large, petal-like eyes. Encouraged by my attitude, Monia enthusiastically went in to cook.

'She takes good care of me,' Lalit babu went on. 'And why won't she? Is there any comparison between *me* and *them*? She cried her heart out begging me to come back.'

At night the radiant moon rode up the sky, and the moonlight, falling on the ancient oak tree and the branches of pine and mahagony trees, cast a spell—transforming the pleasure garden of Benigi into a mysterious landscape of bygone days. I recalled the story of the two lovers—Monia's father and mother who had come away to this place, rejecting society and its norms. They had come here to spend the remaining days of their lives with love as their only capital!

Monia came and called us to dinner at nearly 10 at night. The girl had cooked a huge meal. She had fried a wicker basket full of puris, sitting in a solitary corner of that truly large house. Her pretty face was flushed, her brows moist with drops of sweat in the heat of the oven, her long dark hair hung dank and loose. I felt a strange compassion seeing her thus.

Monia fed us generously sitting beside us. She prepared a hubble-bubble for Lalit babu and brought us both some betel nut and spice. There was no tradition of chewing betel leaf after dinner among the Hindustanis. I envied Lalit babu's good fortune. The good-for-nothing fellow was having the time of his life, attended by Monia day and night! It was enough to make me resentful. Thereupon I resumed my acquaintanceship with Lalit babu and visited the *phoolbaree* in Benigi several times during the month, pursuing the link we had established during my one-year sojourn in Monghyr.

A couple of visits later my appetite for further knowledge about the man increased. Perhaps I was unduly curious, but my impulse was perfectly legitimate, normal in any human being. I was curious about one fact only—the relationship between Monia and Lalit babu. The man could be easily taken as fifty-five or fifty-seven years old. It would not have been an error of judgment on my part had I put him down as sixty years of age. But Monia didn't look a day older than her twenty-four years, even if I were to exaggerate. Was the relationship between the two one of father and daughter, master and pupil or lacking that, brother and sister? In respect of their ages, it ought to have been any one of these. That would have been natural and acceptable to me. But what is proper or becoming doesn't come about in this world—more's the pity!

I must describe what took place to arouse my suspicion one day. It was a hot day and the sun had become scorching. I went over to see Lalit babu at three in the afternoon. I found Monia alone in the house. Seeing me she wailed, 'Babuji, he went out somewhere in the afternoon, saying he would be back in an hour. He hasn't come back as yet… what am I to do?'

I learnt that Lalit babu had gone to a nearby village to buy some *shimul* tree cotton for his pillows. No matter how hard I tried to make Monia see reason, she kept on flitting restlessly in and out of the building, worried and apprehensive. I felt I was regarding Monia anew. I knew that day she loved Lalit babu. Hers was not the love of a daughter for her father, or a sister for her brother. It was romantic love, which only someone who had witnessed it could know.

Then Lalit babu himself divulged a few facts. Monia's name had cropped up in our conversation. He said, 'The girl has whiled away her youth looking up to me…I wonder what will happen to her when I am no more! Society has no use for her. She has no one but me. At times I feel rather sad!'

If someone had told me earlier that a girl of twenty or twenty-one could fall madly in love with a fifty-year-old man, I would have laughed in his face. But I had seen this for myself. What little we know of the mysteries of this world—I was dazed by my discovery of life's many secrets!

I was also struck by another fact. Lalit babu was jobless; he was incapable of helping Monia out with funds. It was Monia who was bearing all his expenses. She had been cheerfully supplying Lalit babu with money all along. Lalit babu supported an unemployed nephew in his village. I knew that because Lalit babu would often ask me to send money by post; there was no post office in the vicinity of where he lived. Lalit babu's life style had also gone up considerably compared with his frugal mode of living in Monghyr. 'It is easy to grow rich sponging off other people,' I sniggered in private. In conversation, I asked, 'How long were you a private secretary to Monia's father? How did you get to know Monia?'

'Would you really like to know? It happened that no one in Calcutta wanted my books; there wasn't a publisher in sight. I came away to Monghyr—that was 12 years ago. An important lawyer belonging to the place told me that one of his rich clients was looking for a Bengali secretary who could write letters in English. I went to see the client, got the job and stayed on for seven years. I moved out only after Monia's father passed away. I took a room in Monghyr, and that's how you found me, when you were visiting here last. Monia brought me back with much entreaty. What could I do?'

Poor Lalit babu! What choice did he have—really? I had seen Monia shadowing him around, eagerly smoothing over any slightest difficulty or suffering in his way. How could I disbelieve what I had seen with my own eyes?

Visiting them through some months, I began to feel Lalit babu wasn't doing for Monia even a fraction of what she did for him. In fact he was doing precious little. He stayed in Benigi not out of any love for Monia but because he was out of work and Monia was taking care of him. He treated her as his menial, ordering her about. At times he even behaved as if he was a well-to-do Bengali gentleman, suffering her presence because he felt sorry for her. There were countless days when, sitting on the broken-armed wrought-iron bench, next to the chameli bush, under the shaded trees of Benigi's pleasure garden, or on the steps of the pond, I brooded over the peculiar tragedy of the young girl's life. Why did such things take place in the world? Why should the beautiful girl, whose small favour any young man would have gladly given his life to win, be destined to suffer?

I was sitting by myself in the garden one day when, observing Monia in the distance, I called out to her. I knew she roamed in the garden at this time every day.

'Why are you sitting here, Babuji?' Monia said, moving near.

'I am happy sitting… is Lalit babu up?'

'No, he usually gets up at four, then I prepare tea.'

Lalit babu's afternoon naps had the regularity of a clock. I had never known him to budge from his routine.

Dusk was descending. Monia was wearing a pale olive-green sari and a blouse cut out in the local fashion. She wore armlets around her fair rotund arms, large dangling earrings on her ears, and a black dot on her forehead. She looked rather like a fairy-tale princess in her old-fashioned clothes.

Like any other girl belonging to these regions, Monia had little idea of what went as fashion.

'Sit down, Monia,' I said.

'I'm okay. I like to stay on my feet. I keep sitting all day.'

'But you like to wander out by yourself at this time, don't you?'

'Oh, I do. He's usually asleep at this hour. I have no work in hand, I like to go out…'

'Don't you, sometimes, take a nap?'

'I don't like to sleep in the afternoons; I'm not used to it.'

'Tell me, how long have you lived in this house?'

'Since my childhood. The house is ours you see—the home of my parents. It was kept so nicely when they were alive. Baba had a real passion for gardening; he planted so many trees with his own hands. He had planted an oak tree whose leaves curl up like little bowls. They say that Krishnaji drank milk from cups like these, which hung from identical trees, growing on the banks of the Jamuna, in Brindaban. We call the tree *bansibat* or the flute tree. Come let me show you…' She led me, across the pond, to a spot where a tree with green leaves, folding up like cups, stood in the middle of the wood. Monia pointed her finger at it. 'See…isn't it strange? Just because long ago Krishnaji drank milk out of cups like these, the leaves still keep folding up. Isn't this enough to cure people of disbelief'?' Monia went on and on, gesturing excitedly with her hands.

I nodded like a sage in assent. 'You are quite right Monia. Absolutely correct!' Who was I to wise her up and destroy her simple faith?

'When did your father die?' I asked.

'Six years ago, Babuji…'

'Where did you live after he died?'

'I lived here, where else? I lived with my dadima and cousins.'

'Where are they now?'

'They all left after he came. What could I do? He was so unhappy in Monghyr. Baba hadn't left me enough money to bear his expenses over there. We manage somehow now that he lives here. I couldn't bear to see him suffer so…I had to bring him back to this place.'

'But your relatives—your cousins—must have been angry with you…'

'Oh, they were…mighty angry. They told me, "Why did you have to bring the Bengali babu here?" I said, "It's my house, I can do as I please." That's why they left. But, tell me Babuji, who else do I have?'

Monia's eyes grew moist with tears. I felt pleased about the girl's honesty, her courage to speak out the truth. I turned the conversation round.

'Can you sing, Monia?'

'A little, not really well.' She answered shyly.

'Will you sing for me—sing a song!'

It hadn't occurred to me that Monia would get me wrong. She gave me a dazed look and said disapprovingly, 'Babuji…' Really, I hadn't the least intention of making any overtures. Nothing I had said had hinted that. But Monia seemed to have misunderstood me. I hurriedly made up for my faux pas.

'Alright, you don't have to sing now. You will when Lalit babu asks you—won't you?'

All along Monia had behaved towards me—her guest—with decorum befitting an aristocrat. She looked so beautiful now. Regarding her clad in old-fashioned clothes, against the background of an ancient, leafy garden, I felt she belonged to the days of yore, and that she would stand out as odd and out of place if she were installed elsewhere. The evening wore on, and a *dahuk* bird, perched on the bough of an ancient oak tree, called. It had become time for Lalit babu to get up.

'Let's go in Monia, it's nearly four o'clock.' I said.

Later in the evening, I made Lalit babu induce Monia to sing for us. She had a melodious voice, even though she sang mostly Bihari folk songs. Listening to her singing I felt as if the Benigi *phoolbaree,* with its rich cluster of mahagony, *krishnachura* and chameli trees, had gradually faded away and I had gone back to the days of ancient India; as if the heroine of Banbhatta or Shudrak or some such poet's epic romance had come to life, and was sitting in front of me, singing Magdhi songs, and strumming the strings of the veena with her delicate fingers.

I saw Monia again that night, in the play of light and shadow of the full moon. I mused at how Banbhatta had created his image of Mahasweta, the heroine of his romance, in the likeness of a beautiful girl like her; how the magic that restores the aged earth to its youthful hues could only dwell in the gentle smile, in the petal-like eyes, brimming with tears, of some beautiful woman like Monia!

Perhaps I was taken with Monia because I was still in my youth. But even today, the Benigi *phoolbaree* with its bower of ancient trees, chameli groves and exquisite Monia come alive in my mind's eye, whenever my thoughts turn to Bihar and to the west.

A month later, Lalit babu came to visit me in Monghyr. I was pleased to see him.

'Come in Lalit babu. When did you get in?' I asked.

'I've just arrived, I'm going home.' Lalit babu wiped perspiration off his brows.

Astonished, I said, 'Going home…to your country?'

'Yes, to my country, I have come away from that place.'

'Come away? What do you mean? How's Monia?'

'She is fine. Staying there has been too much for me! I'm leaving.' Lalit babu added sharply.

'But what's happened? Is anything the matter?'

'What do you think could have happened…I can't stay beholden to someone else forever! I am obliged to send eleven-and a-half rupees home every month. I have been asking her for the money, over and over again, for the past two days, but she keeps on postponing, says she'll bring the money today or tomorrow. Tell me how long can a man continue to beg? She handed me five rupees this morning. I flung the money at her. That woman! She doesn't have to teach me the value of money! My books had gone into three editions at one time. Her mother was a fallen woman. What kind of respectability does her family have? The *chhatu*-fed Marwari clan do not know how to show respect to a decent Bengali gentleman.'

I could take some of Lalit babu's remarks as the words of an aggrieved lover, but not all of it. My good opinion of the man altered rapidly. I remembered how he had been after me to get his books published. He had no interest in literature whatsoever; he was only on the lookout for money.

'But it's possible that Monia doesn't have any money.' I ventured.

'No money! Do you mean to tell me she doesn't possess even seven rupees? That's bullshit! She has behaved in the same way earlier, when time had come to send money home. Besides, it's not only this...Sir, I've had enough of a life among *chhatu*-eating folk. I want to go home, be fed with *mankochu* and rice pudding, prepared with fresh molasses. I want to escape the ordeal of living here—for a few days. Does anyone know how to cook in this place? There's always only one vegetable dish—either with brinjal or with *palval*. How can one live here—for God's sake!'

'Who do you have at home?' I asked.

'Who do I not have! I have nephews, their wives and sons. Does living here counterbalance abandoning them at my age? At home there's nothing wanting—enough is enough! It's time the prodigal returned home. No more of life in the country of *chhatu*-eating breed. I'm about to gasp for breath.'

I felt like asking him that if he was that well-off at home, where was the need for sending money to his nephew every month, from this wretched country? And money grabbed by deceiving an innocent girl. The man was an ungrateful cur!

Lalit babu left by the afternoon train. I didn't feel like seeing him off. 1 was *that* disgusted.

I saw Monia getting down from a tom-tom, from the window, two days after Lalit babu had left. I took her inside and made her sit down.

'Babuji, do you know where he has gone?' Monia asked in an anxious voice. 'Did he visit you? He has been away for almost two days now. He had money with him. He's so absent-minded. I feel afraid...Monghyr is not a nice place, Babuji.'

I was struck by surprise. 'What money?' I asked.

'He had my necklace with him, which he was going to have melted and redesigned, and 50 rupees besides. He said he needed the money to buy cement and lime for repairing cracks in the large terrace where you both sit and have tea. He was to have returned yesterday. I couldn't rest when he didn't get back this morning. Did he come to see you, Babuji?'

I was stunned by the news, but knew not why I couldn't bring myself to reveal the whole affair to her. There were more sorrowful things in life than the loss of money. The innocent village girl would have been hurt beyond measure if she came to know the truth. Perhaps I had become rather soft towards Monia, that's why I wanted to protect her from life's miseries.

I said, 'Lalit babu had to rush home all of sudden, learning his nephew had fallen ill. I myself received the telegram. He took the money along with him in case the need arose. In a hurry, he couldn't do anything about your necklace. He said he would get his village goldsmith to refashion it.'

I didn't stay in Monghyr for long after the incident. Monia came to see me at intervals of six or seven days to find out whether I had heard from Lalit babu, while I stayed. Needless to mention, there was no letter from him.

I didn't visit Monghyr for almost five years to that day. I had left the place in the month of Magh; I went there again after the Bihar earthquake, only to find out how my *pishima* was faring. I shuddered at the destruction I saw. There wasn't a trace of the old town of Monghyr. Everywhere there were signs of devastation, wrought by Lord Shiva's *tandav* dance. And this was three or four months subsequent to the earthquake and the tragedy of Bihar was almost a thing of the past.

After a week, I knew not why, I hired a tom-tom and proceeded towards the country house in Benigi. All through the journey I felt apprehensive about what I would see: a house reduced to rubble, Monia buried under the debris of falling bricks—and that figment of my imagination, the veena of Mahasweta, eternally silent after sending out long wailing music among the shades of the oak, the mahagony and *krishnachura* trees. I was least prepared for what I saw.

The carriage stopped at the gate. On entering the garden, I found the house standing as it always had been, peeping through the gaps in the thick foliage. The place didn't appear at all deserted. Advancing towards the chameli grove, next to the waterless marble fountain, I came across a woman hanging clothes on the washing line, made out of wire. I came to a sudden stop as she, hearing a footfall, looked back in surprise. She was Monia! She looked different now, with added weight and a change in her facial expression. But she was beautiful still.

'Know me, Monia?' I asked.

The look of surprise on Monia's face lingered only for a few seconds. She brightened up.

'Why, it's Babuji! Do come in…where were you all this time? There has been no news of you since you left…I worried so much for you.'

'I wasn't in these parts at all. I got back here only a few days ago. What a terrible disaster it has been for your country! Are you keeping well, Monia?'

Monia nodded her head gracefully. 'We are all alive due to your blessings, Babuji. The house hardly got a scratch. Come, let's go in.'

'Are you alone, Monia? I mean, who else is there in the house?'

'My dadima and my cousins…and *him* too.' She gave me an embarrassed smile.

'Who? Lalit babu?' I spoke out loudly—this time really surprised.

'Who else?' Monia hung her head low and smiled coyly. 'He had gone away, and had lived in his own country for two years. My dadima and cousins came back to stay. He returned after three years had passed, blowing all the money in no time and disposing of my necklace too, but let those things be, Babuji. I was so miserable when I saw him with a long beard, straggly hair and filthy clothes. He has been staying here ever since. His health has improved and I don't allow him to mention his country even once.'

I knew that Lalit babu was no spring chicken to jeopardize his future by mentioning his village.

'Where's he?' I asked.

Monia smiled. 'Come into the house. We are so lucky to have you with us again. He'II be so pleased to see you. He's not up as yet. He'll get up at four, then I'll make tea.

A *dahuk* bird called out from a branch of an ancient oak tree as it did in the old days. The Benigi *phoolbaree* suddenly became an enchanted castle, and Monia a sleeping princess just roused from her slumber. Time had come to a stop.

I felt jealous of Lalit babu all over again.

The original Bengali story was first published in Benigir Phoolbaree, 1941

Bangle from Tirol

Tiroler Bala

Martin and Burn Company ran a small railroad in the up country. Even though it was time for the train to move, the warning signal had yet to go. Passengers, crowding into the compartments, spoke freely about the running of the train: 'Gentlemen, I should be getting off at Barageche, five miles up. It's already four in the afternoon—with no sign of the train starting out, Lord knows when I'll be reaching home!'

'That's how the company runs this passenger train! Come, let's put our heads together and send a complaint to the newspapers. The other day, they packed two compartment loads into one—there wasn't a standing space—yet the train arrived at Kadamtola an hour behind time!'

'The train runs punctually during office hours though, but it's the same story at other times!'

'Oh, how stupid of me to have built a house beside this railroad! I had retired from work and was wondering where I could construct a house. My father-in-law suggested his village as a possibility—'

'Where's that place?'

'Prasadpur—where there's a deity. Childless people go there to buy charms. It's just 20 miles to the further side of Howrah Maidan—not far at all. I had thought the place was nearby and economical to live. My in-laws stay there. Did I know then about malaria and the hassles of travelling? I had spent so much on the house. The train is acting up all the time—this stupid railway!'

'Acting up, did you say? I had always thought this couldn't happen to me—somebody teasing me endlessly! I take the train every day—I feel like weeping at times.'

I was on my way to Chapadanga, the last stop on that particular route. I felt uneasy listening to all the talk. I had received a letter from an aunt, who lived four miles away from the railway station, on the banks of River Damodar, begging me to come and see my dying uncle—perhaps for the last time. The conversation of sundry people made me wonder when I would be reaching her place.

A youth, accompanied by a beautiful seventeen or eighteen-year-old girl, was sitting on a bench in a corner of the compartment. The girl had a flowery silk saree on, Madras slippers on her feet and hair hanging dank and loose about her shoulders. She was gazing outside. The youth was listening to our conversation, looking out of the window and smoking. Soon the train chugged along, leaving three or four stations behind. Itinerant travellers alighted the train carrying bundles of betel leaf, *palval*, potatoes and baskets of fish in their hands. The remaining flock of men seated on the bench, spread their dhoti pleats and played cards, facing each other. Soon shouts of 'Two Hearts!', 'No Trump,'

'Three Spades,' rented the air, piercing the rumbling noise of the moving train. The evening was drawing in, with the palm tree stems picking a reddish glow from the dying sun, when the train eventually trundled into Jangipara station. The train had become near-empty with the last itinerant passenger getting off—but that was not absolutely correct, as I was still aboard, and that youth and his companion were also there. I had made a note of that from the corner of my eye!

I felt quite solitary in the absence of passengers, whose conversation I had been enjoying all this while; my attention naturally riveted to the youth and the girl. She was unmarried—that was an easy guess. But were the two brother and sister, uncle and niece? The girl was rather good looking! Was the youth running away with her? Not unlikely at all—given the character of young men nowadays!

But I quickly abandoned the thought. I didn't feel it was necessary to worry my head over such things—when I had hardly an inkling of what the future held in store for me! With the dusk settling down I became preoccupied with the thought of the hazards of a journey to my aunt's house, some two or three miles up the railroad. By that time the train had pulled up at Antpur, the next stop. It then trundled on, leaving that behind too. I gazed at the dark evening descending on the wide plain land of the western parts of Bengal, at the small agricultural townships coasting the railway track, pumpkin plants climbing up house tops, and people returning home from the village market, resting pots and baskets on their heads. Then I saw more stretches of open fields, bats speeding in the air and descending on the crest of berry trees, fishermen lighting up their torches to trawl for fish in the ditches. Once again I glanced at my companions. They were sitting quietly, looking out of the window.

All this time the two hadn't exchanged a word. I wondered if they had quarreled while making their escape. They were both handsome to look at—couldn't be brother and sister, uncle and niece—of that I was sure. Were they runaways from home? But where could they be heading for? Martin Company's railway terminated its journey in a desolate village, in the middle of an expanse of dryland, extending beyond the horizon in a rural district of West Bengal, after a couple of stops. It was no place or a proper destination for a fashionably-dressed youth and a girl. But I drove away all such apprehensions thinking why should I care?

The green signal had come on in Piyasara station and I had become extremely apprehensive at the prospect of confronting a dark and a frightful night. There had been many instances of theft and robbery on this side of the Hooghly district. I had some money in my briefcase, which *mashima* had asked me to bring for *mesho mashai's* treatment. My mother had given me the money. I began to fear I would fall prey to the dacoits and lose my life.

All of a sudden my youthful companion looked straight into my eyes and said, 'Sir, do you know how far the river is from Chapadanga station?'

'About half a mile.'

'Can one get a boat for the crossing?'

'The river is shallow…but I suppose one could.'

The youth looked out of the window without adding another word. I was curious about where they were going, but receiving no encouragement to continue the conversation, I lapsed back into silence. The youth resumed his enquiry as soon as the train came to a halt at a tiny station, where hardly anyone got in or got down.

'Sir, do you think one can get some transport on the other side of the river?'

'What kind of transport do you have in mind?'

'Any kind—a motorbus or a horse carriage.'

I stared in amazement. What kind of rubbish was the boy talking? Who on earth would arrange a cab for those two in that godforsaken village, I wondered.

'No dear, there is no such means available there, so far as I know. The village doesn't have even a proper road to speak of.' I had consciously withheld my curiosity about those two and their destination, however, the next minute the youth himself volunteered to assuage my desire to know more.

He said, 'Sir, do you know how far away Tirol is from this place?'

I gasped in disbelief.

'Are you going to Tirol? Why, that's very far indeed, not less than 12 miles up—at least that's what I think. I am new to this country, I can't be very sure…'

Signs of anxiety and apprehension crept onto the boy's face. He moved closer.

'You won't mind if I tell you something—will you?'

So…they were running away secretly! Just as I had imagined! But why were they going to Tirol, I wondered. People went there for a different reason. I turned to him.

'Yes, do tell me,' I said.

'I am taking her to Tirol.' The boy whispered in a low voice, pointing his finger at the girl. 'I want to get the bangle of the frenetic Goddess Kali for her. She's my sister, you see. She must wear the bangle on the day of the new moon—that'll be tomorrow…'

I interrupted him, 'Is the girl…'

'She's been calm for almost two months now. She's impossible to control when she is disturbed. I hadn't realised we would get in so late in the night; people had said Tirol wasn't far from the station.'

'Where do you come from?' I asked.

'From an exceedingly far-away place, from the Sailadi coal mines, near Dhanbad. I am not at all familiar with these regions. I have come here only because people advised me to. Now I'm really worried about bringing my sister to this wild countryside.'

I tried to fathom the youth's problem in silence. The poor boy! He was asking for trouble. I gazed again at the girl—she was really beautiful! Fair as snow, with large eyes and lips slightly turned up in the corners, which only added to her charms. Even if the boy were to hire a cab, there was no reason to believe that travelling across a strange country at night, taking along such a beauty, was a safe proposition. The other way around was to stop the night at Chapadanga. But few people there might be inclined to be hospitable or offer them a place when they came to know the girl was out of her mind. Nevertheless, I said, 'Would you rather stay overnight at Chapadanga? Would you like me to look around for a place for you two?'

'Absolutely not, Sir,' The boy was vehement. 'I can't keep her among strangers. She'll get into a violent mood! She doesn't eat unless I feed her. She flies off the handle at the slightest provocation—I can't depend on her at all. If only you saw the state she gets into…it will frighten the life out of you! It makes my blood run cold—I, who am her elder brother! It were better you never saw her like that. She becomes a totally different person.'

In the meanwhile the train had reached Chapadanga. It was early in the night but, with the dark days of the fortnight of the new moon around the corner, it was easy to guess how much darker it would soon become.

Chapadanga station had a few hutments surrounding it. They were mostly shops with thatched roofs, selling betel leaves, bidis, flattened rice and groceries. A cycle-repair shop and a homoeopathic doctor's clinic, with a post office next to it, also stood there. Houses of agricultural labourers skirted the other side of a large pond.

We surrendered our tickets at the gate and came outside. I felt somewhat relieved at the sight of a couple of hooded cattle carts. When I discovered the cattle cart would take us only as far as the river, I asked my youthful companion whether he preferred to stay the night at the station or had some other idea. The cart could not be made to plough through the water!

The youth sounded exasperated. 'But I have to reach Tirol by tomorrow, Sir, the beginning of the new lunar fortnight! It won't do for us to stay here tonight. Do put yourself out for us, this once, please...Come along with us. I can't let you go, now that you are here. What will happen to us if you abandon us?'

I knew I was in deep trouble. On the one hand, I had to reach my aunt's place as soon as possible, with the money I had brought with me; on the other, I couldn't abandon the youth in the perilous situation he was in, with a girl who had lost her mind. No! I couldn't possibly do that, even if it meant I was dispatching my uncle to his fate. The driver of the cattle cart, however, held out an encouraging prospect. He told us that the road to Tirol was paved, and that crossing the river and asking about, we could easily avail of a cab or a palanquin; there was absolutely no danger in travelling to the place. A lot of people visited Tirol, merely two hours away from the river bank, he said.

So we reached the river side, the three of us, sitting inside a cattle cart with a thatched roof. I hadn't heard the girl utter a word all through the train journey; she spoke out for the first time now.

Turning to the youth, she said, 'Dada, I'm cold...aren't you chilly too?'

She had such a sweet voice; it sounded like a wave of melodious notes sent out by a sitar! I gazed compassionately at the girl. What a pity that someone as beautiful as her had come to this world doomed forever.

'You are cold because of the wind from the river,' I suggested. 'Do you have a shawl to wrap yourself with?'

'No, she doesn't,' the youth butted in. 'It's summer time, we haven't brought any shawl with us. We had sat on the train, spreading our bed sheets.' He turned to the girl. 'You can put that around you if you want.'

'Dada, what is this river?'

The girl sounded normal. She spoke with spontaneous ease.

'It's the Damodar river.' I interjected.

The girl now turned towards me. 'You mean the river that flows by Ballabhpur? I recognize it now. A big river, isn't it, Dada? I had seen it before, when I was a child…'

The youth enlightened me, saying, 'Ballabhpur village is situated next to the Damodar river in the district of Bardhaman. It is our uncle's place, you know. Purnima, I mean my sister, has visited the place twice; once as a child and then again when…'

We were about to cross over to the other side, when Purnima exclaimed. 'I feel so frightened…we won't drown, will we, Dada? The boat is rocking so…'

'Why will we drown? So what if the boat rocks? Keep sitting quietly!'

We couldn't see a soul, leave alone find a horse carriage when we crossed over to the other side. The boatman was a good soul. He comforted us, saying, 'Cattle carts can be arranged from the village, I'll go and bring one—wait a while, Sirs—you may keep sitting on the boat.'

'Dada, won't you have something to eat? We have all the food.' Looking at me Purnima added, 'You may also eat, there's so much…'

Dada exclaimed enthusiastically, 'Yes, yes, do give him something to eat and take some yourself. You haven't had anything up till now! We will be reaching Tirol late.'

Purnima unwrapped a bundle and fed us both with *luchis*, fried *palval*, sauted potatoes and *mihidana* sweet.

'I hope *mihidana* has not gone off, just see Dada.'

'Where did you buy the sweet?' I asked.

'In Bardhaman, on our way here. Does it smell bad? Taste some and say.'

I had little imagined an evening like that one or thought I would ever find myself having a meal, reclining on a boat, floating down the Damodar river, in the company of two strangers, a boy and a girl. The atmosphere was so serene! I felt comfortable, as if I was amidst my own family. I began to feel a great liking for the two. But today, when I recall that evening or my youthful companions, pushing back memories of circumstances that led to the agonising experiences that were to follow, I feel it would have been far, far better if I had not met them at all. I would have been spared images of the heartbreaking tragedy that has haunted me since.

We had already had our dinner when the boatman returned with a cattle cart. We handed the driver of the cart the requisite fare for our journey to Tirol, and didn't miss giving the boatman a tip. At the very start of our journey, the driver said, 'Sorry, Sirs, but I have forgotten to bring along my tobacco tin…we'll have to make a detour through the village. You won't mind that, will you? It won't take up too much time.' The cart passed into Shaymakur village, with its mango orchards and clumps of bamboo trees. We saw women cooking, sitting on the raised platform of their houses. We travelled along a wide plain road that lay behind the village hutments and ran in the middle of fields of sugar cane and flourishing jute crops, that extended very far. There were some woods and banana plants here and there. The plains of the western part of Bengal were not thick with vegetation.

'How far from this point is your aunt's place?' Purnima asked me.

'That's not on this side of the Damodar river at all, it's on the other side…four miles down the station.' I replied.

'Then we have put you out, haven't we? I'm so sorry,' she said.

'It's no trouble. I can go to my aunt's tomorrow after you've finished what you have to do and I put you both on the train.'

All of a sudden Purnima broke into peals of laughter, stuffing a fistful of the sari end into her mouth. 'Hi, hi, hi… you're not in trouble…you'll put us on the train, hi, hi, hi.'

I had not seen anyone laugh like that. The beauty and excitement her laughter exuded moved me to no end. At the same time, I felt that her laughter revealed a deranged mind—no level-headed woman would giggle like that in the situation we were in. All at once I felt her brother nudging me in the dark. I knew that something was amiss. I was scared. I hoped to God the girl did not become uncontrollable and, thinking it safer to stay mum, I didn't utter another word. Who knew how the girl would have construed what I said; her behavior had already turned rather peculiar! I began to brood about how her hearty laughter brought fear rather than joy on its trail. The girl was really star-crossed!

Some time passed. We had been sitting quietly inside the cattle cart, which was moving according to its own rhythm—going over wide, open spaces. I had become slightly drowsy when I woke up with a start. I got the feeling a violent altercation was taking place between the brother and sister, inside the hooded darkness of the moving vehicle. I turned back to look as the girl give out a little scream. All along, I had been sitting in the front of the cart, while those two were at the back, curtained off by a mat made out of bamboo slips. The back was obscured from my vision. Before I could say anything, the boy called out to me in a deep troubled voice. 'Hold her, Sir, hold her back. She wants to jump out…' He didn't raise his voice so that the driver wouldn't hear the commotion.

I sat stupefied, wondering how on earth I was to hold the girl back, when I heard the boy shriek out in pain. 'She's bitten my arm. Don't touch her, don't…'

By this time, the driver had brought the cart to a standstill. Looking up at us, he asked, 'Gentlemen what is the matter?'

I had little time or the opportunity to fashion a suitable reply as the girl was pushing hard at me, trying to come out in the dark. The brother shouted, 'Take her by her hair…don't touch her. She'll bite you.' But before I could do anything, the girl, throwing me aside and advancing to the front of the cart, had fled into the darkness. Both I and her brother leapt out of the vehicle. The bewildered driver barely had time to bring the yoke down from his shoulders. Even though the night hadn't turned pitch black, we couldn't trace the girl in the midst of the open field. I was at my wit's end and, so was the girl's brother. Our driver, however, showed a lot of dare and sagacity at a time like this. He had already had a good guess at the situation. Everyone knew that people who visited Tirol had a person in their midst who was not quite in her/his right mind. The driver probably didn't suspect who that person, among the three of us, was. He said, without wasting time, 'Switch on your torches, Sir. The Patihal canal is nearby. We can't afford to lose her there.'

We had become so thoroughly confused that neither of us remembered that the boy carried a torch in his pocket. Following the driver's footsteps, both of us ran like mad. Moving swiftly over vast stretches of open field, we reached the edge of a narrow canal, bound by thick bushes on either side. We looked for the girl everywhere, combing the thick clusters, shouting on top of our voices. She was nowhere to be seen.

Everything had happened quite suddenly, at almost lightning speed. We had hardly given a thought to the seriousness of the situation, or to the adverse circumstances that could easily overtake us. Purnima's dada was almost in tears. 'Is there any other canal or ditch in the vicinity?' he asked.

The driver said, 'There's no other waterway near about this place. But why don't one of you wait beside this canal while two of us go and look for her?' I opted to stay behind and remained standing beside the canal. I had sensed the young man was not inclined to hang about alone in the dark.

They had gone away when I realised I hadn't even a box of matches with me. I wondered how long I would have to wait all by myself, in the darkness of the approaching fortnight of the new moon. I can't remember how long I waited, perhaps an hour or more when, moving away from the edge of the canal, I walked towards the open field. I was mystified by the non-appearance of the other two. Suddenly, I saw a light flickering in the distance. The voice of the driver calling out 'Babu, babu…' entered my ears. Hearing me respond, some people from the village could be seen approaching—one had a hurricane lantern in his hand.

'What happened?' I asked anxiously. 'Have you found her?'

The person carrying the hurricane lamp said, 'Come along with us, Babu, they are all waiting for you in my house. Know what, Sir, I had gone inside the cowshed late in the evening to prepare fodder for my cows and what do I see—but a breathtakingly beautiful lady sitting in one corner of the shed. I was so stunned. "What's this?" I say to myself. Soon people in the house trooped in; those two also arrived. We have put them up and have come to look for you. What calamity for a gentleman like you, Sir, to get stranded in the dark! Come to a poor man's lodging, Sir, have a proper meal. The sister of ours is the incarnation of Goddess Lakhsmi, if only she were mentally balanced. But she has rested her feet in a poor man's abode. I hear you are Brahmins. We would have prayed the length of our lives for such luck! Please take rest in our place tonight. I will take you to Tirol in my cart tomorrow morning. It can't be otherwise.'

I reached the man's hut walking through the village. It is necessary for me to describe the house in detail, at this stage of my narrative. What happened next is closely connected with the way the house was built. Sometimes I think if only we had gone to Tirol straightaway and had not agreed to put up there for the night—I wouldn't have had the terrible experience I had had! But we humans are all driven by fate. We do what we do because of it. I couldn't have escaped what was in store for me even if we had left for Tirol that very evening. It's a mistake to think I had a choice.

The house where we were put up had mud walls and a thatched roof—common to that region. There was a largish living room in the exterior part of the building, partitioned by a thick wall. A big raised platform ran all the way in front of the house, facing an even larger courtyard. A small pond, with stone steps, lay to its west. The smaller room of the two didn't open to the courtyard; it led to the interior of the house.

The householder was known as Rasiklall Dhara. He was of Kaibarta (scheduled) caste. Not allowed to cook for us, he entreated us to prepare our own meals. He dumped all kinds of ingredients for cooking in front of us—milk, vegetables and the lot. To my surprise Purnima volunteered to cook. She was back to her normal self, was quiet and peaceful. Hearing her talk, observing her behavior, and noting her culinary expertise, no one would have guessed that she had jumped out of the cart and had run away only a short time ago.

I peeped into the kitchen before sitting down for the meal. I found a lot of village womenfolk crowding around her, asking her all kinds of questions. Purnima's notoriety had become well-known, I guessed.

Purnima called us to dinner at 11 in the night.

'Have you met all the people?' I asked.

'Do you know why they were here? They had come to take a look at me,' she answered shyly. 'I told them, 'What is there in me for you to see? I am a girl like any one of you. I have two hands, two feet…"

'What else did you talk about?' her brother interjected.

'Not much else—they asked where we came from, how old I was and all that…' Then, assuming a familiar tone she added, 'And they were asking whether I was married. I told them my father was thinking of marrying me off this year.'

She was serving me some dal—I looked up at her in amazement. Her brother gave me a wink. She could be mad, I thought, a raving lunatic—that didn't mean she was not driven by desires, natural for any woman. I felt quite miserable. I knew the unfortunate girl would never be able to achieve what she craved for. But apart from such minor faux pas there was nothing in her talk or her behavior one could fault her with. She was *that* normal. Her voice was as sweet as honey. I couldn't remember ever listening to such a charming feminine voice! No one could have mistaken her for a commoner either. She moved with such grace and behaved so decorously.

Purnima looked at me, 'We have put you in such a wearisome situation, Dada, you must visit us at Sailadi once.'

'That'll be nice. I'll come, of course.'

'You must come during the Puja festival. We celebrate two pujas in our place. One of them is organized by the colliery officers, the other is held in the market. Amateur theatre groups come there to perform…'

'You must watch the Santal (tribal) dance too. It's worth your taking the trouble, Sir. Do visit us during the festival season. That'll make us happy to no end,' her dada joyfully added.

'Then, that's settled. You are coming. You can't refuse a sister's invitation, can you?'

The householder came in with some milk. He asked Purnima to give us some to drink. Turning to a girl, Purnima said, 'Go, bring me another spoon, child. I can't serve milk with the spoon used for dal, can I?' I remember bits of the conversation like these, very well indeed. There was a good reason to mull over them during the ensuing events. We had gone to bed half an hour after we had had our dinner. I slept in the large room, Purnima and her brother in the adjoining smaller one.

It is time I disclosed the state I was in that evening. I was physically exhausted and mentally fagged out and had dropped off to sleep almost at once. Suddenly, I knew not why, I was wide awake. I felt someone was pressing a heavy object down on my chest. I couldn't breathe. At first I thought I had caught a chill—with the cold wind blowing in from the riverside, it was more than likely. As I tried to go back to sleep, I heard a rather curious noise coming from the room next to mine. I took it to be the sound of snoring. But the din was too loud to be mistaken for grunting. After a while the noise ceased, and I turned to my side and went off to sleep.

I was awake rather early the next morning. I found the door of their room tightly shut. I got up, washed, and went out for a stroll. I returned half an hour later and to my surprise saw no one about; neither the youth and his companion, nor the people of the household. Sometime later, Rasik came out and sat on the platform. He asked, 'Did you sleep well? Were you bitten by mosquitoes. Err…they are not up as yet!'

I chatted with Rasik till he left me and went out; it was almost 8 o'clock then. Neither the youth nor his sister had risen from their sleep. Rasik was back at about 8:30.

'Aren't those two up?'

'They are still asleep,' I said, 'They couldn't have slept well last night, it was so hot. I guess they are making up for the lost hours in the morning.'

My narrative is coming to an end. Hearing no sound coming from the room even at 9 o'clock, I knocked at their door. It seemed as if there wasn't a soul within. I was compelled to peep in through the tiny window to the west. I noticed the girl lying. I felt awkward about prying like that but what else could I have done? I simply had to find out what the matter was.

I must have cried out loudly at the sight from the window—I say I must have, because I have no clear recollection of the moment. I was so greatly befuddled that I was hardly mindful of the scene I had witnessed. There was blood just about everywhere. My curiosity aroused, I wondered if my eyes were not deceiving me—but that lasted only a second. I saw Purnima's dada sprawled on the wooden bed, lying in a peculiar position on his stomach. The bedding was soaked in blood. Blood was streaming all over the place, also on the floor. Purnima was seated plonked against a wall. I couldn't tell, from that distance, whether she was alive or dead. A cushion, detached from the bedding, had fallen on her body. It was red with blood.

My cries must have pierced the air; neighborhood people came rushing in. In the meanwhile I had lapsed into unconsciousness. It took them a while to bring me round. They had to break open the door and enter the room. Purnima's dada had deep gashes on his neck, arms and shoulders, produced by the sharp knife Purnima had borrowed to cut vegetables with the night before. The knife, covered with blood, was lying abandoned at the edge of the bed. Purnima's clothes, her sari or her blouse, were not stained; they bore only a sprinkling of blood shots. I realised that the woebegone girl had committed a dastardly crime. She had killed her brother with her own hands and was now lying on the floor, lost to the world. But I couldn't find a trace of anxiety on her face when I entered the room. She looked so beautiful in her slumber, so innocent—the picture of an unblemished beauty. All of a sudden the terrifying image of Kali, the Goddess of destruction, floated in my mind's eye. I recalled how Kali had the power both to destroy and create. She carried the sacrificial dagger in one of her hands while with the other she bestowed love!

The ensuing events were as expected. All hell broke loose, and the police arrived. I revealed to them what I knew about the girl. By the time the cross-examinations were over and done with, I had begun to feel that I myself had committed the abominable act. I had to arrange moving the brother's body from the girl's side, extirpate other signs of the crime—the bloodied garments, the bedding and the knife. It was a relief the girl had not stirred, her dormant insanity was not roused.

Actually, Purnima slept peacefully till noon. The police could wake her up only after a great deal of exertion. I came and stood beside the girl in the dark. Who else was there to stand beside a lost soul? However, those who came, the men and the women, shed tears at her pitiful condition. The Muslim police inspector of the area was visibly moved. A telegram was sent to Sailadi without delay and her father arrived with three of his friends. I came to know from them that Purnima was married: her husband wouldn't take her in because she was mad. At times she remembered she was a married woman, at other times she did not. Purnima's mother was no longer alive. I realised her father was not willing to take her back; arrangements were made to admit Purnima to the Ranchi Mental Hospital. She was brought to Howrah station in a car straight from Sri Rampur court. When we were about put her onto the Ranchi Express she gave me a wide grin.

'You must come and visit us at Sailadi, Dada, remember?'

She turned to her father, 'Where's Dada, Baba? Why can't I see him. My ears feel so bare…he has my earrings.'

All these incidents took place some years ago. You understand what it means to recall them—People disappear but their memories remain…Lives get lost—sink deep into oblivion but the faint traces of the footsteps of one's near and dear ones remain hidden in the depths of the sand bank of memory. Whenever I think of how Purnima was banished from this verdant earth, the glorious sunshine and the palpitating change of seasons, I feel she couldn't be alive. By now the wretched girl must have ended her cursed existence in some lunatic asylum in distant Ranchi. How long would God have allowed her to suffer—tell me?

I don't have to mention that I have used fictitious names and places to tell you this story…and for a good reason too!

The original Bengali story was first published in *Benigir Phoolbaree* 1941.

NASU *MAMA* AND I

Nasu mama ebong ami

When I was a little girl, barely eight years old, Grandma would say, 'I'll marry you off to that boy Atul.'

We were staying in my maternal uncle's house. Father was what one called a *ghar-jamai*—a live-in son-in-law. I came to know that much later, as I was growing up. Atul was the son of Grandma's childhood friend. A rather tall and fair-complexioned boy, he went to school somewhere. He would sit and chat with Grandma in the kitchen. The way he talked—I didn't like him at all. He would say, 'Ei, Panchi… get off from here, go and play in that corner,' or 'I'll throw you in front of the long-limbed wolf in the bamboo forest if you behave so naughtily.'

Everybody said Atul was a nice boy. He did well in studies and got promoted to a new class ever year. He spoke in English to my younger uncle. I had no idea what they talked about. Perhaps that's why I never took to him, no matter that he was good boy and was liked by everyone.

I liked Nasu—the boy from the Mukherjee household. He was so good looking! So fair complexioned, with soft and round-shaped limbs, large eyes and a smiling face. He was slightly older than me—not as old as Atul though. Atul *mama* was sixteen or seventeen years of age. Nasu had such a lovely smile, with teeth flashing like pearls—he reminded me of Grandma's stories. I hadn't seen such a lovely face in all my eight years in that godforsaken village. He came and chatted with Grandma too. He uttered sweet nothings, and 1 took in whatever he said, open-mouthed in wonder. Atul always tittle-tattled…how was it I was never turned in by his talks?

Grandma said, 'I'll give Panchi away to Atul in marriage. They look nice together.'

I sat glum-faced. 'Nice? What rot!'

Grandma laughed. 'O dear, what does the girl say…why won't you suit each other?'

'You know everything, don't you?'

'Then what is it you have in mind? Who'd you like to marry?'

'That Nasu.'

Grandma rolled over laughing. 'The girl has already chosen her groom! A sign of the times.' Turning to her friend she said, 'Have you heard, Sister, Nasu is to be her husband!'

Atul's ma smiled. 'Why, dear, why is it that you don't fancy Atul?'

'Atul *mama* is too old!'

'He isn't that old—just sixteen years of age.'

'Doesn't matter…why must 1 marry an old man of sixteen? Nasu is a young boy.'

Grandma said, 'Look at what the girls of this age are up to, friend…she likes Nasu because he's only twelve years old. Times have indeed changed. 1 was thirteen when I was married, and he forty-two. He took me in as his second wife. And you…'

'He wasn't that old—only thirty-nine and I was eleven…

'But you were a second wife too, weren't you?'

'Not only that…his first wife was still alive.'

'Well, God has saved me from that ordeal, and that is a blessing!'

At times, I wouldn't see Nasu *mama* for days. He wouldn't come and play in our quarters. My heart would pant with longing, and I would rush to the Mukherjee house.

I would find Nasu *mama* in the courtyard, surrounded by boys of his own age, splitting bamboo stalks to make a boundary wall for his make-believe house.

'O Nasu *mama* why haven't you visited?'

'Why must I go everyday…but you've walked all this distance? Aren't you afraid?'

'No.'

'Will you play with us?'

'Yes.'

The boys would immediately protest, 'Why must a girl play with us—go, go and play with Puti or Manti.

'Let her play with us—how does that matter?' Nasu *mama* would break in.

'Can she split bamboo stalks with a chopper, what game can we play with her? Go, now!' Habu would insist. Seeing me about to weep, Nasu would come and hold my hands.

He would tell the boys, 'Why are you all after her, why should she chop bamboo? She's a girl. She'll sit quietly—sit down Panchi.'

I would immediately go and settle in the corner of the courtyard, Nasu *mama* would fling me a guava in the middle of his playing, I would sit and eat. After a long time, I would say, 'Nasu *mama,* I'm hungry.'

The boys would pipe up, 'Listen to her, such bother!'

Nasu *mama* would shut them up and ask me 'Are you hungry? Come, let me take you to *Pishima*'s. You can have some flattened rice mixed in oil and salt. I'll pluck you a tender cucumber from the tree.'

'I don't want it. Take me home—I will eat rice at home.'

Habu would pucker his brows. 'How did you manage to get here all by yourself that now you want us to escort you home? Who's there to accompany you, you wicked girl?'

Nasu *mama* took me home many times in those days. Piles of earth, excreted by worms, lay strewn by the wayside of the dusty road. Birds congregated in the trees; ripe fruit lay fallen under the *bakul* trees. I was very fond of the *bakul* fruit. I yearned to pick some up and give them to Nasu to eat. But he said, 'Hang it, it has an acrid taste. You eat, I won't.' Nasu never gave me the chance to be happy seeing him eat.

My childhood and adolescence passed, like some cool Chaitra morning, reverberating with bird calls, under the shadows of the familiar trees of my uncle's village home. Then, as life moved on, my days became harsh—sun-scorched—and those dawns of springtime, of blossoming flower buds and bird songs, gradually faded away. The air became hot.

That old village—Taghra Shwkharhati is still there. I go there sometimes. How the place has changed! My uncle's house doesn't exist anymore, my grandma is no longer alive.

Father worked in someone's warehouse. He earned a pittance. There were constant fights between him and Grandma about how to run the household. Father would leave the house in a huff, not send us a word for a month or two, make Ma weep, then turn up, all of a sudden. Days would pass.

I was married off when I was thirteen to a man belonging to a village next to Arangghat. I had gone to Nasu's house a few days before my wedding. I found Nasu boiling rice in the kitchen, his pale face red in the heat of the oven. Nasu's mother was unwell, and Nasu was doing all the cooking. He had several brothers; some worked, others went to school. With a continually-ill mother, Nasu had had to take over the kitchen chores. I had long noticed that there was no just distribution of labour in that household. I felt really sorry for Nasu. No one cared about him. His brothers were a selfish lot, burdening him with all household responsibilities

Seeing me, Nasu laughed. 'Come Panchi, come and sit. I'd laid some yoghurt yesterday, it hasn't set as yet—should I place the pot next to the oven? What do you say?'

What a lot of girl talk Nasu indulged in! No wonder people said he was the widowed daughter of Janardan Mukherjee!

'Do you know I roasted and crushed some moong dal yesterday. It took me the whole afternoon...I have such aches and pains all over my body now,' Nasu said.

'Really! You roasted the moong dal?'

'Yes, dear—who's there to do it? I'll have to boil a pile of dirty clothes in soda and soap tomorrow.'

'All that is woman's work, Nasu *mama*,' I said, in a sad voice, 'Why should you undertake it? Why didn't you call me—I would have roasted the dal for you.'

'Come on…why should I call you? There's nothing in the world I can't do.'

'But won't you ever learn how to read or write, Nasu *mama*? Go to school? You are a man…this kind of work is not for you. You must study.'

'Who'll send me to school? My dadas won't spare a penny for that. Besides, Ma is not well, who'll do the cooking if I go out of the house? I don't think I can study even if I have money.'

I sat and chopped the vegetables for him, told him I was getting married. Nasu *mama* hardly showed any interest. I would have felt happy if he had—asked me who I was getting married to. But he didn't say anything. Such happiness was not in my fate. Nasu *mama* joined the wedding feast and ate to his heart's fill but didn't once peep into the bridal chamber or attend the wedding ceremony. I felt a strange emptiness in my heart. It would have been so nice if he had appeared. I was not so grown up then as to delve deep into my feelings, yet I knew something was missing. I didn't enjoy all the food, the music, the new clothes and ornaments, or the rush of people. I remained totally unenthused.

My husband was barely seventeen or eighteen; he was thin and balding. I learnt he was an old malaria patient, and that he come down with fever routinely, twice a month. My uncle-in-law ran a sweet shop during the fair held in honor of Jugal Kishore Thakur. My husband sold sandesh, *murki*, as well as toddy there.

It was not that I was not curious about my in-law's household when I first went to them. I had wondered what their house would look like, what food they ate etc. I arrived to find the house was an old-fashioned brick-built hut, with two rooms, a small veranda and a cemented platform, that ran all the way in the front. The kitchen was also a hut. A huge, crouching mango tree had pushed the courtyard into shade.

My mother-in-law said, a hint of pride in her voice, '*Bouma*, it's time for mangoes to ripen—you'll see—there's not another in the whole locality to compare with ours. The master has built this famous garden with his own hands, planted seeds and saplings brought from so many places: Goari, Shantipur etc.'

The mango season arrived; traders came and bought the garden. A couple of mangoes, from a basketful offered to the family, came my way. My mother-in-law was not boasting—the mangoes were really good.

I got to know my husband rather well, became fond of him too. He asked, 'What do you like to eat?'

I wasn't a bit shy, and said, 'Fries.'

'Hang it, such a stupid girl! Can't you think of something nice?'

'*Gaja*, jilepi.'

'What about *khaja*?'

'What's that...I've never heard of it.'

He roared with laughter. 'A real country bumpkin, you are! Listen...this is a small mofussil town. I'll bring some *khaja* for you secretly tomorrow. Take care, Ma must not get to know about it or she'll scold us. I sell *khaja*.'

From that day on my husband would occasionally and unobserved bring home sweets which we two would eat. On days he would bring *khaja*, on other days, *mihidana*. He said, 'We can't afford to give sweets to everyone—my cousin brothers are as numerous as a gaggle of geese. There won't be a piece left to lift to our mouths if we stuff them with sweets.'

I didn't care about my in-laws, but I had this soft spot for my husband because of the food. The locality didn't put up a fair as big as the one in Ullor, the sweet shop always remained busy. My husband got home invariably late, carrying huge packets of sweets. He would smile and say, 'Eat, eat to your heart's content—come, let us both.'

My aunt-in-law remarked, 'Such a piggish lot! They deserve to be given a few lashes of the broom. They have cleaned out the shop eating. And I haven't come across or heard of such a shameless bride—not one bit embarrassed about gobbling all the food behind the backs of her elders.

At night, I said to my husband, 'Don't bring me anything, anymore...See the fuss they are making!'

Husband said, 'Why won't I? Does uncle pay me for the work I do? He treats me like an unpaid servant. Can't I fill my stomach with some food? Of course, I can...I'll bring some again for sure, you'll see! I dare uncle to find me out!'

My husband didn't keep at all well, yet continued to eat voraciously. He never listened to me, brought loads of left-over *luchi*s and rasgullahs every night. Stealing food from the shop didn't cease. Although never free of stomach ailments, he didn't pay heed to my warning him not to indulge in eating. He would say, 'I eat to make good money uncle owes me. Not a penny will ever slip from his fingers.'

❧

'I'm going to visit my parents in the month of Ashar. Won't you buy me new clothes?' I asked.

My husband puckered his lips, 'Who's there to buy you new clothes? Uncle? That'll be the day!'

'Really, won't I get new clothes? Everyone in my family will be slandering me.'

'You would have got everything had I the means. Do you think I don't feel like buying you clothes? How can I—how can I afford to?'

'I'll have to put up with all the criticism then.'

I came home in Ashar; my husband accompanied me. Womenfolk of my age, in the village, had nasty things to say about my husband when they saw him. One day, the second daughter-in-law of the Ray household, called me in and said. 'I believe son-in-law mixes toddy in the sweet shop.'

I didn't understand what she was getting at. 'He makes excellent *khajas*. Everyone praises his skill in preparing *khajas*.' I said.

Mejoginni killed herself laughing, conveniently forgetting that her eldest daughter-in-law was reluctant to leave her parent's home because she was in love with the boy next door. My husband's job at the sweet shop became the object of her ridicule, and the target of her verbal brick-bats.

The village folk also showed no respect to their new son-in-law. I felt sad my husband was slighted by everyone when, as a new member of the community, he should have been welcomed and fed.

I found Nasu cooking as usual. Sitting and chatting with him was the only thing I could enjoy. I noticed Nasu had become quite taken with religion, even though he was so young. Seeing him pounding sandalwood into a paste, I asked, 'Does Grandmother perform puja these days?'

Nasu laughed. 'It's me who does the puja, not Ma. I sculpt images of Shiva and pray to them every day so that I may be reborn as a human being and make a pig of myself eating—'

I was amused to hear him utter this fundamental truth. He gave me cut cucumbers and sweets made out of coconut to eat. He offered me tea.

A couple of years or more passed this way. My husband's health did not mend, rather, it went downhill. Both my mother-in-law and aunt-in-law said, 'The unlucky bride is the reason why our boy hasn't stayed well for a single day.'

'Haven't you noticed she's not attached to anything in this household?' My mother-in-law added. She hadn't said anything wrong. It was true I had little fondness for things. I didn't have any taste for fine clothes, jewellery, anything at all.

My husband said 'Why don't you save a bit? Put aside what I give you—from time to time—it will stand you in good stead in the future.' I hardly paid attention to his words. What was the use of thinking what the future held for me?

I had given birth to a boy; he died a few months later. My husband remained perpetually ill. I worked liked a dog in the house, but no one had a kind word for me. My husband gave me all kinds of worldly advice. 'He was so frail, he may die any day, what's to happen to me then? I should put aside some money…' I would keep his words in mind when I heard them and soon forget everything about it.

That year, I came over to my parent's place in the month of Magh. I heard that Nasu *mama* had gone off his rocker. He prayed day and night, didn't speak to anyone, and had become rather strange. I went to see him that very evening.

'What's all the news, Panchi, when did you get in?' he asked.

'Yesterday…are you keeping well, Nasu *mama*?'

'I'm very well, I'm happy!'

'But everyone says you've gone off the rails.'

Nasu *mama* gave me a faint smile and went silent. Then, looking at me with steady eyes he said. 'I'm looking for the *real* thing—It doesn't matter if people think I'm mad or stark raving…Hi, hi, hi, O dear Panchi!'

My regard for Nasu *mama* went up in leaps and bounds although what he said at the end seemed rather incoherent. His expression had turned rather peculiar. But I discovered something in him I didn't find in an ordinary individual. All around me, I saw how people clung to their money and property, how my aunt-in-law raised the whole village with her tantrums if a boy so much as picked up a mango lying under a tree in her grove, how lawsuits were carried on for two or three years if someone in the village extended his boundary wall by a yard. Nasu *mama* stood out as a distinct human being in such an ambience. He had no interest in clothes, in food or any material thing. He had given away all the property he owned to his brothers, without asking for a penny.

My husband came over to our village for a few days. I had developed quite a soft spot for him. No one seemed to care about him save my mother-in-law, but she was too old and her words hardly carried weight even with my uncle-in-law. Our village too had no use for him. He had no standing there.

He said. 'It'll be nice to build a house here.'

'Why must you live in your in-law's place? What'll people say?'

'Let them say what they like—I don't enjoy staying at my uncle's anymore.'

'Give it a thought.'

'People in your village are a peculiar lot, they don't know how to speak.'

I was angry. 'Who respects a man who makes toddy?'

My husband gave a wink. He smiled. 'Oh, you don't seem to mind when it comes to eating *khaja* every night.'

My husband went away after a couple of days. He gave me coins worth 13 annas before he left. 'Buy sweets with this money—do. Stay on here for a month. I will come and fetch you after that.'

He never came…he left this world at the end of the month, died of his old stomach ailment, rendering the sindoor in my hair-parting and the conch shell bangles clasped around my wrists totally redundant. Baba had told no one about it when he first received the news in a letter. A couple of days later he told Ma, 'There's something I have to tell you…son-in-law is seriously ill. I have a letter.'

Ma was worried stiff. She said, 'What's this—why haven't you said anything till now? Did you receive the letter in the market? Let me see it.'

Baba spoke out hesitatingly, 'Yes, I didn't remember—it's not that, I mean…'

I had pricked up my ears and had heard everything from the next room. My heart was thumping blood into my brain. My throat became dry. I knew at once all that there was to know. Baba was over-particular; he was not the person to keep quiet at news of his son-in-law's illness. Ma ran panting to him. 'Go there at once, go and see him. Haven't they asked for the girl? Take her along…'

'What's the use of going there, wife? It's all over,' Baba said in a withered voice.

Ma threw herself on the ground and let out a cry. But I took the news rather calmly. I had already anticipated what Baba had to tell me.

My married life ended thus. What could I do—it was in my fate. No blame to anyone…After all, Baba hadn't married me off to a doddering old man, he had found someone young for me instead. I was not particularly unhappy. I didn't feel I had lost something or that I lacked anything. People said my life lay in shambles; I couldn't fathom what they meant. True, I wasn't allowed to eat fish but I didn't mind that. I was ready to go on a fast on the 11th day of the lunar month. I was never interested in eating well or dressing up, but I had become quite fond of my husband. I was sad I wouldn't see him again.

I visited my in-law's place several times in my widowed state to take care of my mother-in-law, especially as the old woman was miserable, compelled to stay with a scold of a sister-in-law. I tried my utmost to make her happy. We fasted together on the 11th day of the lunar month, I rubbed oil into her feet in the evenings. My aunt-in-law never stopped saying I was the unlucky wife because of whom their darling boy—the lamb—had to die early. I couldn't remember her ever expressing such sentiments for her nephew while he was alive. Strange indeed!

One day, visiting my parents, I heard that Nasu *mama* had left home and was missing. Six months later we came to know he was involved in worship and had put himself up in a temple on the banks of the Ganges in the town of Halisahar. The mother of Buddha, the neighboring milkman, brought us the news. She had met Nasu on her way back from the Ghoshpara Holi festival. 'Good for him' I thought to myself. I had always felt that whatever Nasu *mama* did was becoming. I kept my mother-in-law safe with love and care, hardly staying with my parents lest she faced hardship. Days passed this way.

'Come, Ma, let's go to Sanyal *mashai*'s house to listen to the Bhagavat Gita,' my mother-in-law said one day.

'Who is he, Ma?'

'Haven't you seen the old man, the elderly gentleman in our locality?'

So we went over to Sanyal *mashai*'s house. He seemed quite well-off from the look of things. I heard that Sanyal *mashai* was a widower and that his two sons lived and worked in Calcutta with their wives and children. Sanyal *mashai* declared to us that he was seventy-six years old. His widowed sister stayed with him and cooked. He received us warmly and interpreted the Bhagavat Gita to us.

We began to visit Sanyal *mashai* quite often. He was very affectionate towards me. A book on the fundamentals of meditation and the Gita were his favorite reading. He would turn up at my in-law's place if I absented myself even for a couple of days. He regarded my mother-in-law as his daughter-in-law. Coming to our place he would call out:

'O daughter-in-law!'

My old mother-in-law would cover her head and respond, 'What is it, Dada?'

'Where's Nirmala (my proper name)? Call her at once.'

I would come in and ask. 'What's the matter, Grandpa?'

'Why call me Grandpa, I am your elder uncle! I'm eleven years older than your father-in-law. Why haven't you come to my place for so many days? You must certainly be there today.'

Thereafter I went over to his place every day. I found Sanyal *mashai* no longer interested in having others listen to his interpretation of the Gita, he was happy to have me as his sole audience. Lord knew what he saw in me! His recitations wouldn't take off if I was not present.

One day I asked him, 'Uncle, I am only an ignorant female. What is it you expect of me?'

'Lord knows!' He said, 'I little know what to expect but my Gita and yogic meditation come alive only when you are present. Their words carry new meanings. If discussion of the scriptures are a means to eternal bliss, then I get full measure of that when you are here.'

I laughed, 'Say then, Uncle, you never found an audience like me, ever?'

'That's true…I didn't know how explaining the scriptures to another human being could fill me with so much happiness. I had been reading the scriptures to myself. Now I understand things differently, I know that the right audience makes all the difference…'

I too enjoyed going to his place. I had begun to feel differently about life. I had never cared for family or home and now I became even more detached. All that tied me to the world was an old mother-in-law. She would weep all the time and I would expound the philosophy of deep, abstract meditation to her. It hardly gave her any comfort, she was far too worldly. She continued to fight with her sister-in-law over her share of *sajne* stalks and jackfruit even in her old age. I would tell her, 'Ma, what's the use of squabbling over portioning the jackfruit or the *sajne* stalks? What do you achieve? Turn your mind to God!'

The pompelmoose turned ripe in the Spring month of Phalgun, scattering its sweet smell. The ground underneath the clumps of bamboo trees got covered with flowering *ghetu* shrubs. Abstracted by the song of the cuckoo, I thought of so many things—my childhood, Ma and Baba and my husband—I had everything, although I seemed to have got nothing out of life. Perhaps I wouldn't have been able to show anything if a person who computes life's blessings had asked—nothing beyond a dirty, thin-bordered saree and the much-worn couple of slim gold bangles I wore. He wouldn't have known about the state of my heart which was a storehouse of unending happiness! All else paled to insignificance in its face.

One day my mother-in-law said, 'O *Bouma*, a boy from your village has taken up work at Hari Kolu's house…a handsome-looking Brahmin boy! But why should he be fetching water, or cutting grass for cows at the Kolu household, what sort of thing is this? Perhaps he is very poor. Haven't lighted my eyes upon him…people assembled on the banks of the pond, were talking…They said he came from your village.'

I came upon Nasu *mama* on the road the very same day. I couldn't recognize him at first. His hair had grown long, he was wearing a saree half-covering his head, he had bangles on his arms. He was dressed like a woman, although he was sporting a faint stubble on his face. I felt like laughing at his bizarre get-up. He spoke out in a womanish voice, 'Ei Panchi, are you keeping well, friend?' I was stunned. 'How odd you look Nasu *mama*.' I said.

Nasu *mama* laughed in a strange manner. 'It'll do…'

'I hear you scrub pots and pans, draw water from the well for the Hari Kolu household…'

'What's wrong in that?'

'Do as you please.'

Old mother-in-law left this world in the month of Shraban. Suffering from high fever for days, she looked up at me, her eyes full of tears, minutes before she died, 'Who am I leaving you to, Ma?' she said. I was pained at the tone of distress in her voice. I folded her frail hands into mine, 'I have my gold bands, a bigha of *aman* rice field as well. I have nothing to worry about. You must not be so anxious on my account.' Assuming a worldly attitude I was thus able to reassure someone to whom only tangible things made sense. But inside my heart I knew I belonged to One who had given me shelter at his feet and who would never abandon me.

I met Nasu *mama* again; he was going to the river bank carrying a pile of washing. I said, 'Let me launder the clothes for you—I shan't allow you to do this kind of work.' I took away the clothes by force and washed them clean myself. I was determined not to stand by and watch Nasu *mama* work his fingers to the bone. 'I'll sweep clean Hari Kolu's cowshed too,' I told him.

'No, Panchi dear, what'll people say?'

'I don't care!'

'But I do.'

'That's fibbing. You scrub their pots and pans and yet…'

'You won't understand any of this, Panchi… you mustn't…'

Sanyal *mashai* was keen to meet Nasu, when I told him about it.

There was a pond at the back of Hari Kolu's house, girdled by a mango grove. We found Nasu sitting there under a tree, with his eyes tightly shut. Nasu became friendly with Sanyal *mashai* on that very day and joined his meditation group. Sanyal *mashai* said, 'The boy is a pure soul!'

Cholera made an appearance in our village at the advent of winter. 18 people fell ill, five died. Nasu *mama* took care of the sick in earnest. Hari Kolu's younger brother didn't die only because of his nursing. Nasu never slept. He cleaned the bodies and the beddings of the sick with his own hands. Kolupura was devastated by cholera. Soon it raged in the village of the cobblers. Many fled the place out of sheer fright. Old cobbler Haru died. People were so full of fear that they left dead bodies lying in houses for whole days. Nasu *mama* carried the bodies all by himself on wooden rods to the burning ghat in the evening. I became very agitated when I came to know about it during our meditation session. I decided to go and help Nasu *mama* no matter what people said.

Uncle smiled at me. 'Ma, you can't do this kind of work. The work is not fit for everyone.'

'But am I not old enough to have earned the right to do such work?' I asked.

'Your old mother-in-law is dead—but aren't there enough old people left in the world for you to take care of?'

'I want to go uncle, please persuade Nasu *mama* I'm fit for the job. He doesn't want me around.'

One day, suddenly, Nasu left the village. Everyone in Kolupura bemoaned his absence. My aunt-in-law said, 'Thank god, he had the sense to leave at last. He has made all of us, Brahmins, a laughing stock. Shame on him!' Then turning to me she smiled. 'He belongs to a daughter-in-law's village. You're sad aren't you, that he has left? You would see him all the time...He turned up here, perhaps, because someone from his place lived here!'

I straightened up like an unstrung bow. 'Of course I'm sad he has left...what do you expect?'

One day Hari Kolu came over to Sanyal *mashai*'s house. He said. 'It's hard to find another person like him. I had hugged his feet and implored him not to do all the laborious jobs after my younger brother got well. "You are after all the son of a Brahmin?" I had said. But he left soon afterwards without taking two months salary due to him. He just went away. I hope he will forgive me.' Hari Kolu gave a salute to Nasu in his thoughts.

It's springtime all over again now. Flowers are blossoming in the woods, the roads are echoing with the chirrup of the nightingales and the riverbeds are diffused with the sweet fragrance of *mukchund chapa* flowers—only I am a destitute. I go to uncle's place to listen to the philosophy of meditation every afternoon. Perhaps one can reach *that* place stripped of everything in life.

The original Bengali story was first published in *Upalkhanda*, May 1945.

Fakir

Icchu Mandal was down with a bad cold. His wife, Nimmi, had thrown a patched-up quilt over his torso in the early hours of a chilly Bhadra morning of ringing rains. Ill with a cold, he felt dull and listless. Stretched out on his back, Icchu rocked the rice pot; the pot was usually kept within range of his feet. 'I'm not working today. Can I have some water to drink?'

'How can we manage if you don't go to work?' Nimmi asked.

'Why not—there's some rice inside the pot. Boil *sajne* leaves and spinach to go with it. Do we have salt in the house?'

'There are a few grains left at the bottom of the coconut shell.'

'What's the problem then? Give me some water, let me do my namaz.'

Washed and clean, Icchu settled down for his morning prayers. Icchu had remained very fond of this job since he was a child; he didn't care about earning money, and he never began his day without his namaz.

'Why not go to work since you are up and about? They are paying 10 annas to each person because of the war. You get a measly sum of three annas normally. But you must choose not to work because you have discovered rice in the house—now that's bad!'

'Be quiet, will you? Stop nagging me when I'm performing my namaz.'

Coming out of the house at the end of the namaz, sickle in hand, Icchu stopped in his tracks. 'I'm so hungry—what's there to eat, dear?'

'Nothing.'

'Take a look inside the pot. I'm really famished!'

'There's nothing but a few grains of rice soaked in water.'

'Serve me that. I get really hungry by noon if I don't have something to eat early in the day. My hand shakes holding the scythe…I can't work.'

The rail track ran next to the Shailipara village. Across it, lay an open field with a swamp in the middle, brimming with heavy monsoon water. Water reeds along its edges had begun to blossom, while the aquatic plants criss-crossed all over its liquid surface. Glossy creepers, with ripe red berries peeping from behind their leafy green curtain, hung low and swayed from the tops of wild date trees. A forklined passerine bird swung from the overhead railway wire. The cowherd, Ram, was harvesting his own crop with the help of day labourers. He noticed Icchu.

'Where are you off to?'

'I am going to Sanekpur to gather crops.'

'How much do they pay each labourer?'

'A rupee and 12 annas for a bigha of land…can I have some fire to light my tobacco?'

'Take some from the earthen pot lying next to the prickly bush.'

'I rushed after a meal without pausing…can't put my mind to work unless I take a drag.' Lighting his chillum, Icchu walked ahead, puffing.

The autumn crop had ripened and fallen to the ground in the 150 or 200 bighas of land, a couple of miles away from his village. With the onset of the monsoon, the water overflowing from the swamp would soon drown the ready rice stalks. That's why the labourers' rates were high in the region. The labourers were also provided with their daily rations.

Icchu loved to listen to stories about Allah. The fakir from Pairagachhi was the sole holy man in the region. Icchu had seen him only once. He had been drawn to Allah since he was a child; the fakir only intensified his craving for the Lord. An encounter with him made Icchu more odd. He lost interest in home and family, or working for money. He became indifferent to food, and became absentminded while gathering the harvest. People teased him. 'O Icchu, have you become a fakir after all?' Icchu kept silent, didn't utter a word. He was a simple soul, not given to argument. He couldn't bargain for better rates; many people got their work done by outwitting him. At times he worked for free.

'O Icchu, how can the pumpkin scaffold collapse while you are around?'

'Why…what's happened, Uncle?'

'The poles have all but given in.'

'I'll fix them later in the day.'

Icchu would always keep his word, everyone knew he would try his utmost to do what he promised. The money-lender made over two or three mounds of rice if he so much as expressed a wish. Icchu never conned anyone of money or rice.

Icchu had, by mistake, once harvested crop belonging to Mukherjee *mashai* of the neighboring village—it wasn't a lot—ripe rice stalks of a *kattah* of land, perhaps. His own two bigha of rented land lay next to it. Mukherjee *mashai* made a racket when he got to know about the theft, but couldn't figure out who the culprit was. Being the harvesting season, every household had piles of rice stocked in their godowns. Mukherjee couldn't fix the blame on any individual. Icchu appeared at his doorstep after a couple of days.

'What brings you here Icchu?' Mukherjee asked.

'Salaam, Babu, I've made a grievous error.'

'What is it?'

'I've cropped and stored rice from your land. But Babu, I will return it to you with one-and-a-half times the interest.'

'Oh, so it was your doing Icchu? I was wondering who in God's name was the thief.'

'It was me, Babu. It was raining hard, I couldn't make out the boundary of the land. I said to myself I must go and tell him, when I heard you were looking for the man who had stolen the rice. I will give you one-and-a-half times more the amount since I have unknowingly made you suffer the loss.'

Mukherjee believed what Icchu had to say. Nobody in the place regarded Icchu a thief. He was a day labourer, but the people held him in high regard. Mukherjee said.

'You don't have to give me any interest or return the rice you have taken—consider I've given you that. What's to be done if you have made a mistake?'

'But I can't accept the rice, Mukherjee *mashai*, you must excuse me, please. The rice won't go down my throat. I'll manage with what Allah has deigned to lift into my hands. What he hasn't is forbidden in the scriptures.' Icchu stood folding his palms in reverence.

Mukherjee was pleased, he knew Icchu well. 'Let that be Icchu, go inside and ask your aunt for some flattened rice grain…'

Icchu arrived at the Sanekpur swamp only to find that none of the day labourers had turned up for work. He didn't like that one bit. He didn't approve of labourers taking higher rates and arriving late for work or cheating their masters. He himself worked like a clock, never shirked labour.

A passer-by asked, 'What kind of rice is this?'

'*Benajhupi*.'

'How's the harvest this year?'

'May add up to 50 or 60 mounds…'

'A bigha.'

'Can't be *kattah*, can it?'

Icchu roared with laughter at the wayfarer's ignorance. He shouted back, 'If a *kattah* had yielded 50 mounds of grain we wouldn't have slaved as day labourers, would we have, Mister? Ha, ha, ha,'

'Where do you live?'

'Shailipara.'

What's your name?'

'Icchu Mandal.'

The afternoon train trundled past on the distant rail track. The owner of the rice field had sent food for the day-labourers. Walking the distance from Sanekpur village, a person now appeared—bell-metal pots hung aslant his shoulders—carrying warm rice, pumpkin curry and fried shrimps. Supplying good food at this hour was a ploy on the part of the masters to keep the labourers happy and get more work done.

'I'll leave a bit early today, I have to buy salt,' Akha Mandal said, chewing betel leaves. 'There's no salt in the house, the children won't be able to eat.'

'Where'll you find salt? There's no salt to speak of in the entire market—I had looked for some yesterday!'

'O dear! A salt-less diet has ruined my taste buds!'

'And eating in the dark makes me drop off—I haven't seen the face of kerosene in days!'

'The pumpkin concoction was really good. The Sanekpur people give you enough to eat—good food. But now—where will you get kerosene?'

Having eaten, Akha Mandal propped a piece of tobacco on top of his chillum and handed it to elderly Ramjan Mandal.

'How many scores of years have you, Uncle?' Icchu asked.

'I used to mind the cattle in the year of the double floods—some 30 or 40 years ago,' he said.

No one could fathom what he meant. No one knew when the double floods had taken place—how far back in years. Ramjan was easily past seventy years of age, even if one calculated on the low. The present lot of labourers could not have been born in the days he herded the cows. The labourers were weak in numericals though.

The day was about to run out. The five o'clock train chugged by, crossing the swamp to where the cucurbitaceous plants were blossoming in the fields of Sanekpur. Noali Sirdar belonged to the tribal caste. Affluent among the people of the locality, he was proceeding along the village road, herding a battalion of cows.

Seeing Icchu get up from his namaz, he asked, from across the fence, 'O Icchu, can you get me some workmen tomorrow?'

'No, I cannot.'

'Why not?'

'The Sanekpur rice field is being cropped.'

'Come to my house then, take a drag.'

Icchu called out to Ramjan Mandal. 'Uncle, let's both go to Sirdar's house to take a pull at his chillum.'

The real motive behind Sirdar's hospitality was bargaining on the labourer's rates. With Icchu being as young as his son in age, Ramjan could easily assume the tone of a leader discussing the labourer's rates.

'Can't bring it down to less than seven *sikka*s—Sirdar, you mustn't be annoyed.' Ramjan said.

'Then why not maul me to death under your feet, Ramjan chacha?'

'Have I said anything wrong?'

'Haven't you—from 14 annas to seven *sikka*s? Try to think coolly...settle for five *sikkas*, and I'll give you rice, dal and pieces of fish breast to eat. You won't eat out of our hands...but there's such big fresh fish in our pond this year...' Noali Sirdar stretched out his hand to convey the size of the imagined fish, in the hope of beguiling them to agree.

Ramjan firmly shook his head. 'Won't do, Sirdar, Not a pice less than seven *sikkas*...'

'Come take another pull at the chillum, Chacha; pluck some tender cucumber from the climber, eat, both of you...'

'Are you growing cucumbers? Which variety, the one that crawls on the ground or the one that climbs all the way up?'

'Where's the land to grow vegetables, Chacha? I had put up a thatched covering in this very courtyard so that I can grow all kinds of beans and cucumber plants. I don't have money to buy them in the market—prices of vegetables have skyrocketed!'

'Don't mention that...I used to buy two to three seers of brinjal for a pice, it costs eight annas a seer now. There's nothing one can buy now, no people who can afford to eat. Do you grow zucchini?'

'By your blessings I do. I'll pluck some for you.'

'No matter...let's settle for five *sikkas* as rate then, Sirdar, but don't divulge the fact to anyone.' Having had a pull at the chillum, Icchu and Ramjan got up to leave with cucumbers and zucchini. Noali Sirdar got what he had wanted. He knew that Ramjan was the leader of the union of labourers. He fixed their rates. He had to be kept happy.

Icchu was late getting home. He asked Nimmi, 'Have you cooked?'

'I don't feel too well this afternoon. There's some rice soaked in water, you can have that.'

'What about some vegetables?'

'There are none.'

'Cook some of this zucchini then.'

'With what? Where's the oil? I had borrowed five ladles from Achhiran bibi the other day, and I haven't paid her back as yet. Must I run for more now?'

'Roast them.'

Stuffing her saree end into her mouth, Nimmi burst into a fit of giggles. 'Mother of God, where can I look...I've never, ever heard of roasted zucchini. You won't be able to swallow it!'

'I can—serve me some.'

They finished their meal, cooked on a wood fire. There wasn't a drop of oil in the house. Darkness reigned indoors; one couldn't make out who came in or who went out...But outside, the glow worms made waves of light in *kochu* bushes and clusters of screw pine flowers; beams of brightness moved up and down. Lightning struck in the skies, like the dazzling smile of the gods, presaging rain. The heat of the month of Bhadra was suffocating. After the day's back-breaking work, Icchu drowned in sleep the minute he fell on the mat. He was soon lost to the world.

Icchu was rudely woken by people's commotion. He had no idea how much time had passed; the voices of so many people gathered in the courtyard came to his ears.

'What's the matter?'

Old Hafez, the headman of the village, called out to him.

'O Icchu, are you at home?'

Bachhiruddin Shaikh said, 'O Icchu, get up and come here.' It was day break. The birds had begun to chirrup. Icchu scrambled out of bed and rubbed his eyes. The time for the morning namaz was about to run out. But why were there so many people assembled in his courtyard? Why were they calling him at the crack of dawn? Gazing at the courtyard with sleepy eyes, he was struck by surprise—the entire village had congregated there. Astonished, he asked, 'What has happened?'

'Come here,' Old Hafez Mandal said.

'Let me do my namaz, it has gotten late.'

Icchu came outside after completing his prayers on the platform at the back of the house. The entire crowd of people came forward now, as if to say something. Icchu became apprehensive, his heart began to thud. He felt frightened. Where had Nimmi gone at this hour? What had happened? Interrupting the rest of the menfolk, Hafez said, 'Come with me.' Icchu followed Hafez like a wound-up doll. Everyone was marching towards the train track. Wading through knee-deep water in the marshy field, all of them came up to the track and drew up behind a date bush.

'Come here,' Hafez repeated.

What could be the matter now? Icchu's head reeled at what he saw. He took hold of himself, about to collapse. A bloody body lay on the track. It had a deep gash in the throat; the head was scrunched up in an awkward position against the rest of the figure. It was Nimmi's body.

Icchu's mind went blank. He couldn't remember what happened afterwards. Village folk, collecting together, asked him so many questions—where was he, how long was Nimmi away from the house and so many other questions. Nimmi hadn't killed herself, sticking her neck under the running train; someone had murdered her, dragged her body and thrown it on the track. There were signs. People were beginning to suspect him, Icchu realised. They had gone to his house to ascertain where he was and ask him questions before they went to the village overseer with the news.

Icchu sat down cupping his head. 'I don't know anything, Chacha—Allah knows—I was sleeping like the dead…'

'Did you scold your wife? Was there a fight between you two?'

'Nothing of the kind, Chacha.'

'Did your wife sleep in the room?'

Icchu was suddenly stung by a strange suspicion. Why were people asking him such odd questions? Bachhiruddin Shaikh pulled him up and said to the others. 'Listen to me, all of you, Icchu is not *that* kind of a person. We must take him immediately to the pleader in Bongaon. He'll do what needs to be done. We must seek his advice. The overseer will get hold of him if he hangs around here. Let some of us take him to Bongaon right now, solicit advice before the police arrest him. Who among you is coming with me?'

Almost everyone wanted to go.

'But how can I scratch up money to pay the pleader?' Icchu asked in a hoarse voice. 'I have a rupee which I had put by for tomorrow's expenses...would that be sufficient?'

'Why worry your head over money? Your life is more precious to us than all the money in the world. Leave the matter to us...Come along with us...What do you say, Bacchiruddin?'

'Why, of course, you must not think of money—the problem is ours.'

'Let us walk along the rail track, we'll run into the police if we take the main road.'

They reached the house of Ramlall Chatterjee, the senior pleader of Bongaon, at 7:30 am sharp. Ramlall babu hadn't been up for long. He was in his records office, having tea and scolding his clerk for being late, simultaneously. 'Yesterday you left the kutchery for home without bothering to collect signatures for the two bail bonds. You turn up at eight, now! How can I work if you go on like this? Have you picked up the transcripts of the petitions?'

'I've applied for the two transcripts, Sir—Binoy babu left early, I missed him.'

'Go and get the transcripts out from the court early in the morning. There won't be any hearing otherwise...Who's there? Where have you come from?'

Hafez Mandal went near and salaamed Ramlall babu.

'What's the matter? Where are you from?'

'I have come to you, greatly troubled...entangled in a murder case.'

Ramlall was an old hand in law. He had gone grey pleading on behalf of the defendants. He knew people went on a spending spree when the case was tough. In those situations he had to realize his fees, keeping his head cool. He lit a cigarette. Though old in years, Ramlall babu never pulled at the hubble bubble; he was addicted to cigarettes. Taking a smooth drag he said, in a grave voice, 'Murder? What kind of murder?'

Hafez pointed his finger at Icchu. 'His wife was discovered, cut by the throat, beside the railway track last night.'

'What's his name?'

'Icchu.'

'Where was he last night?'

'He was sleeping in his room.'

'Was she of good character?'

Hafez kept silent. He was the elderly headman of the village, but he couldn't bring words to his mouth. Standing next to him. Bachhiruddin cleared his throat.

'Not good, Sir.'

Icchu stared at Bacchiruddin's face in amazement. Was Nimmi a bad woman? How was it that he didn't have a clue—he was her husband, yet he didn't know what the others did.

Hafez continued to stay mum while Bachhiruddin rambled on.

'Babu, this man is harmless. He hasn't committed the crime.'

'How do you know that?' Ramlall said, giving him a good snub. 'Will people call you up as witness when they commit murder? Speak out the facts only…don't talk big! Now go and sit there.'

He turned to Hafez. 'Tell me what you know about it.'

Bachhiruddin's plight made Hafez feel somewhat scared. Taking control of himself, he spoke out deferentially now. 'It is legitimate what you say, Sir, but our Icchu is an extremely good man. Everyone knows that…ask any person, all will say the same thing.'

Ramlall Babu drew in his cigarette. 'Present the facts of the case.'

Hafez described the circumstances surrounding the incident he had gathered from Icchu. Icchu had gotten home after the day's work and had gone to sleep. Icchu had told him how he had slept the whole night like a log, completely oblivious of what had been going on. His wife had served him rice before he retired to bed. They hadn't had a fight.

'Not a case of suicide, is it?'

'No, Sir, the gash in the deep of the throat doesn't indicate that at all. Someone has cut her throat and thrown her body on the railway track.'

'At least that is the likely presumption…the police will also be saying the same thing. Who discovered the body?'

'My brother and Nobi Shaikh, Sir. They had gone fishing in the canal next to the train track. They saw the body and came running to me with the news. I immediately rushed there…'

'Enough, I understand…you may stop. Let the local investigation be completed first. We'll then see what can be done…. Have you informed the overseer of the village?

Good! It's a difficult case. Icchu, no doubt, will be the prime suspect. The wife wasn't of good character. In the circumstances even a man of gentle disposition can suddenly lose control over himself, do something terrible in a fit of rage. Have you come here undercover?'

'Yes, Sir.'

'Let me teach you something…Icchu!'

Icchu came forward and salaamed the pleader. His legs shook.

'Now, listen to what I have to tell you…I won't ask whether you've committed the crime or not. That's not our business. We will assume you haven't done anything wrong, but the police are not likely to believe that. They will arrest you the minute you go on the road. They will try to make you confess. You must not, under any circumstances, tell them you have killed her—must not admit to anything you've done or not done. Understand? You may go now, but be careful!'

'Where'll the police keep him when they arrest him?' Hafez asked.

'In the lock-up…until the hearing is over. But that won't be the end of the matter. The case will be transferred to the Sessions Court in Jessore where the judge will pronounce the verdict. Go home and arrange for the money. You are in deep trouble, a lot of money is at stake.'

Listening to Ramlall Babu's talk, Hafez and Bachhiruddin felt like sinking into the ground. How could they, the poor villagers, raise funds to pay lawyers' fees in the Jessore district court, when they could hardly scratch up enough to cover the expenses of pleading in Bongaon? It seemed to them that saving Icchu was going to be extremely difficult.

At this point Icchu broke his silence; all this while he hadn't uttered a word. 'Sir I have something to say,' he said, folding his palms. Everyone's gaze turned on him, not excluding Ramlall's. The pleader thought the man was about to spill the beans—confess his crime. It was always this way. The pleader had had enough experience of that. Hafez and Bachhiruddin looked at each other. They wondered what secret Icchu had kept hidden from them. One couldn't make out a man by his outward appearance, they surmised. The pleader Ramlall looked up at Icchu with eyes full of curiosity—as if to say, 'Come now, out with it...we have dealt with many artful dodgers...so now we have you...'

Icchu fell down at Ramlall's feet.

'Sir, I have a request to make, please see that it is granted. I am a poor man, a day labourer. I may not be able to pay you your fees but I'm sure that Allah, who is the Lord of the Universe and of the poor, will bless you if you keep this small request.'

'Oh, dear!' Ramlall exclaimed, 'Keep away from my feet.... don't touch me. Say what you want.'

'Sir, I don't care where and how I am kept in custody, but you must see that I am able to do my five namaz a day there. I have nothing more to add.'

Taking a cue from the classical novelistic mode, we might say that Ramlall couldn't have been more astounded had lightning struck his records office. Hafez and Bachhiruddin rapidly exchanged glances. The wily pleader stared at Icchu full in the face, his mouth open in astonishment. He hadn't anticipated words like these from a village rustic, booked for murder and about to be dispatched to the Sessions Court; a person who had had his full share of trouble, financial loss and physical tribulations while the stern edict of law hung over his head, like the sword of Damocles, pointing to a cruel and bloody fate.

Ramlall Chatterjee recounted the incident to his Bar library associates in the evening. 'I was really amazed when I heard what he had to say, brother. I could never imagine a person about to face arrest, making such a request. He was at the point of losing everything, waiting to be taken into custody. I had thought he was readying to make a confession... He is such an ordinary man! Tears came to my eyes.'

Icchu and the rest left the place together. On the way he was fed with all kinds of fries, samosas and puffed rice. Hafez rued, 'We should have given him a decent meal in a hotel—who knows, he may not get proper food where the police keep him.' But they couldn't find a single hotel open at that early hour.

They walked along the road, all of them together. It was not yet noon. As Icchu sat down to pray under the shade of a wayside banyan tree, he lost count of the happenings of the day. His heart became filled with rare joy and peace as a gentle breeze blew in while he did his namaz. Tears welled up in his eyes. Nimmi had cooked for him so many times, she had taken such good care of him... Was she a woman of loose character? He didn't know a thing about it. His heart stung with pain. Why would he kill her, he had never thought of killing anyone. Allah was a witness to all his deeds. Allah would dispense justice.

The police didn't arrest him while he was on the road. He found the Inspector of Police, the village headman and the overseer, all waiting for him at his house when he arrived there, at two in the afternoon. People thronged to the place, and there was much clamour. By late afternoon the deposition made by the witnesses were complete. The people of Sailipara declared in one voice they didn't believe Icchu had committed the crime. One witness deposed that Icchu's wife was in the habit of leaving home at night after Icchu went to sleep. She had no dearth of lovers, and there was much love-rivalry going on. The Inspector called Icchu and bombarded him with questions.

'You didn't know your wife was a woman of easy virtue?'

'No, Inspector Sir, I didn't know anything about it.'

'Do you realize you can be hanged if you make a false statement in a case like this?'

'If Allah so wishes…I won't have any regrets. He'll do what he wills. It cannot but make me content.'

Old Hafez moved near, and standing up straight, spoke out in a strong and clear voice now. 'Who are you speaking to, Inspector! He weeps at the mention of Allah. There's not another person like him in this place.'

'Where were you last night?' the Inspector asked Icchu.

'I was sleeping in my room, dead to the world. I had worked the entire day in the marshy fields of Sanekpur. I woke up when these people came to call me in the morning.'

The Inspector had had a great deal of experience in the police force. He could distinguish between the guilty and the innocent. He knew, from the look on Icchu's face that he could not have committed the crime. The truth had dawned in the Inspector's heart as clear as heaven's writ.

Icchu felt an immense emptiness within him when, finishing his evening namaz, he entered his deserted, broken-down house.

'O Nimmi...serve me some rice,' he cried.

And he began to call out to her over and over again in his mind. He had loved Nimmi so much; he didn't believe a word of what people said. Who was there to pronounce judgement on her? In his heart he had forgiven her.

'O Nimmi, Nimmi dear...won't you serve me some rice?'

The next day the village couldn't find Icchu in his house. He had left—gone away from the place, as he was, lord knew when.

He had cast behind all his household items: a water pitcher, pots and pans, a string of coconut shells and a few brass jars and bowls.

A fakir has come to the humble cottage on the banks of the river at the edge of Khalsekhali village. People gaze with astonishment at the mild light radiating from his visage when he spreads his date palm mattress to do his namaz, in harmony with the movement of the evening clouds against the firmament of the blue skies. The light is akin to the soft glow of the evening star caught in the radiance of the full moon.

The original Bengali story was first published in *Upalkhanda*, May 1945.

Travelling Salesman Krishnalal

Canvasser Krishnalal

No matter how hard he tried, Krishnalal couldn't keep his job. He had been whirling to and from Sealdah and Barasat, on the Down Khulna passenger train, every day—morning and night (10:45 Calcutta time)—a tin suitcase in hand, like 'a spinner at a yarn,' yelling continuously on top of his voice: 'Oil for rheumatism from Dattapukur—oil for rheumatic pains, swellings, open wounds, sore gums—in a word, all kinds of pain, inflamation and bites will disappear overnight with one application! Everybody taking this train for the last twenty-four years knows about its medicinal value.' Yet Krishnalal got the sack.

Mr Nrityagopal Bose, the owner of the Indian Drug Syndicate, called him in and said, 'Why haven't you deposited last night's cash?'

'If you permit me to say, Sir, I couldn't—it had gotten very late—the Khulna train was 20 minutes behind time.'

'Look here—haven't I warned you at least 17 times earlier? The Khulna passenger gets in at 10:21. I waited in the office till 11:30 last night—only for you! Nitai went twice to the station to confirm—the train had arrived on time, not a minute late!'

'I was rather unwell last night, Sir.'

'Your old story! I'm not buying it this time—forget it—have you brought the cash?'

Krishnalal looked up at his boss with guilty eyes.

'I'll go and bring the cash—err, there's a problem—can I go?'

'You may go.'

Seeing Krishnalal still standing about, Nrityagopal asked, 'What's the matter?'

'Sir, I will bring the money later in the evening. I had kept it in my room. The person I stay with has locked up the place and gone out.'

'Where were you?'

'Oh, I had gone for a stroll in the Goldighi area—'

'Rubbish—I don't believe you—and you know very well why! The cash is deposited after 10 at night. You've become old in the job yet you behave as if you don't know the rules.'

'Of course, of course…'

'Tell me, how many times has it been that you have acted this way? It's impossible to believe a word you say—I'm sorry about this. I've tolerated your faults because you are our old employee—I can't anymore. You may quit work—collect your pay for the past few days as soon as the office opens—and leave the commission behind, will you,—now go!'

Krishnalal hadn't wanted to give up his job that easily. He had pleaded with Nrityagopal, had even gone to his superior, the old man, and pleaded his case. Nothing had worked. The problem was that one can't hold down a job which was as resolute and pitiless as a death-bound traveller journeying to his goal. It was 2:30 in the afternoon when all this happened. Krishnalal had spent most of the day pressing people in order to save his job—he hadn't bathed or eaten.

Krishnalal had been living in room number 17 in the western part of a tall, two-storey, unbaked building with a tin shed, that faced a public urinal constructed by the municipality at the entrance of 25/22 Ramnarain Mitra Lane, for the last 11 years. He didn't live alone, but shared the room with three others—three grimy beddings remained spread on the floor. Entering the room, Krishnalal saw Jotin lying asleep. His other roommate, a tram conductor, normally came home, off from duty, for exactly half an hour at 4:30 in the afternoon; he then dressed and went out, lord knew where. They had arranged to have their meals at a cheap restaurant below.

Jotin woke up on hearing Krishnalal.

'Why so late?' he asked.

'How does that matter—I lost my job today.'

'What! Such an old job.'

'I had entreated my boss so much not to sack me. No one cared to listen—who pays attention to what the poor have to say?'

'What had happened?'

'I couldn't deposit the cash in time, he accused me of filching.'

'So that's what it was—what's the way out now?'

'I'll have to look around for a job again, I'll find one or another—if one door is shut in our faces, a thousand others are bound to open—who dares rob us of our livelihood?'

Krishnalal still had some money. He had a simple meal of dal and rice at the cut-price restaurant and rested awhile. Then, going across to a small uncovered house in Nabin Kundu Lane, he shouted, 'Golapi, O Golapi!'

The person who came out responding to his call presently, was a graceless, middle-aged woman, wearing a dull maroon saree. She had a few glass bangles around her wrists, a pair of gold-plated waist bands hugging her hips. She was fair-complexioned, although her hair had greyed. But had one seen Golapi 30 years ago, he would have had a good idea of how fantastically beautiful she was. Hardly anything was left of it now. Krishnalal was employed as a travelling salesman of medicines then—no one could ignore his handsome looks or his attractive manner of speaking—money had kept flowing in.

Krishnalal had met Golapi while visiting another house in Nabin Kundu Lane with a friend. He was in the spring of his youth, and had a pocketful of cash. Golapi was then, perhaps, sixteen or seventeen years of age; her beauty struck people dead on the streets. Golapi's mother piled up money year after year. Krishnalal became a 'resident by night' in Nabin Kundu Lane. He has remained one ever since.

Their story involves so many years—a chest of drawers of mahagony wood was placed in Golapi's room, a long mirror of foreign glass was stuck on the wall, bottles of popular macassar oil made a riot on her table. Residents of neighboring rooms envied the rows of potted *malati* plants adorning her balcony. Cash jingled in Krishnalal's fist. He brought in three rupees each day; never less than rupees two and fifty.

One day Golapi's mother whined, 'No matter what you say, my Golapi frequently tells me she would like a place of her own—but is she fated for it? We live among a crowd of sundry people—'

'Why is that Ma, why worry about it? I'll look around for a room tomorrow…'

'How much can you spare? We can easily find a room in this neighborhood.'

'As much as you may want—20 or 25 rupees?'

'There's a nice place going for 30 rupees—maybe we can take that.'

'Of course—why ask?'

And so Golapi and her mother came to live in their new house. Old Panchi, the senior resident, said, 'Go slow, dears…be careful the cord doesn't snap. Golapi, you have such luck! Our old gentleman Ray comes here every day and places his false teeth in the glass bowl. I have asked him so many times for a *dhakai* saree and a cuckoo wall clock. The clod, at death's door, has been beguiling me for seven months now. Let him come today—I'll see how he manages to take off his false teeth and place them in the glass bowl!'

But for Golapi, the house was just the beginning. She acquired a table-harmonium, a collection of sarees, a gramophone too—what comforts did she not enjoy? Every Sunday, Krishnalal would take her out in a carriage, (a horse carriage to be sure), to Kalighat to bathe in the Ganges or visit the temple of the Goddess. Years went by.

Golapi and Krishnalal, Krishnalal and Golapi—they were together and inalienable!

In the meantime, Golapi's Ma, ascertaining that her daughter was happily settled perhaps, left for the heavenly regions of Urbashi or Tilottama, breaking free of her ties with Nabin Kundu Lane. The scale of the ceremonies during her funeral surpassed people's expectations. Gradually, Golapi's youthfulness began to fall away. Krishnalal's income tumbled down, and hundreds of imitations of oil from Dattapukur showed up in the market. The train compartments became crowded with ever-new salesmen. Krishnalal had to split what had been previously his own. He was less well off. This was 10 or 12 years ago. In those years beautiful Golapi had turned into an unattractive middle-aged woman. She had had to leave her house and settle in with seven or eight companions, all over again. Nevertheless, no matter the earnings, Krishnalal's evenings were hers. Golapi knew that—in the 30 years she had been with him she hadn't once abandoned him or gone to another man.

'I've lost my job, Golapi,' Krishnalal came in and said.

Golapi was astonished. 'How's that?'

'Bara babu was angry with me for not depositing the cash yesterday.'

'What did you do with the money?'

'It got spent.'

'How did it get spent? You haven't given up your bad

habits—have you? So, why would they keep you? Where had you been?'

'It's not like that Golapi—Don't you remember, I had to borrow money to go to Dakhineshwar? Hadn't I taken the money from a *kabuliwallah*? He caught me at the gate of the railway station last night and demanded I return the dough. Fearing he might stab me, I immediately handed him the cash. It's not nice to be in the clutches of a *kabuliwallah*!'

'You deserve what you've got! Now tell me, have you eaten or not? Fate must conspire to make me your maid servant, I can see! Haven't I told you so many times—'Bannu, let's go away and make a home in the village.' But no—you must stay in Calcutta—'I can't live anywhere else'—your constant refrain. See now, what Calcutta has done to you? Who will feed you in this place?'

'Something has got to give…there's nothing to worry about.'

'As if everybody is waiting to employ an old codger like you—can you hold forth or gesticulate like you did before?'

'I'll show them, Golapi—would you like to see me demonstrate? 'Well, gentlemen—this is the famous, original, unadulterated oil from Dattapukur. All kinds of rheumatic pains, headaches, tooth pain, scabs, open wounds, burns—will disappear with…'

'Enough of that, my lord,' Golapi started laughing. 'You don't have to show off—everybody knows you talk well—and my, my, the way you throw about your hands as if you were on the stage!'

'Tell me then—won't they give me a job?'

'Did I say they wouldn't? A 100 times they will, I tell you. Let me go now and earn my bread working as a maidservant. You can't feed yourself—how can you provide for me? I rue the day you came into my life—'

As Krishnalal was preparing to leave, Golapi said, 'Stay a while—let me mix some puffed rice for you, have some tea.' Krishnalal gave in; he sat down.

'So you agree I'm a good communicator still!'

'Come on—stop fussing. Of course you are—you'll puff up with pride if I tell you that.'

'Tell me if I am, Golapi—please—you must.'

'No one can hold forth like you, dear! Haven't I seen the others—salesmen peddling toothpastes and medicines—those unfortunate vendors at the mouth of our little street, dancing and discoursing with harmoniums down their chests! You are a cut above them!'

A note of annoyance crept into Krishnalals voice. He stopped her. 'There's absolutely no comparison between *them* and *me*. I really don't know what to say to you! Those are petty hawkers, we—the salesmen. Are we to be lumped with them who sing and dance, tying bells on their feet and strapping an accordion on their shoulders? I feel insulted when you talk like that.'

'Sorry—it's my fault. Calm down now—have some tea.'

Golapi was feeling rather happy today. She was seeing Krishnalal gesticulate, listening to his powerful, charming voice—after such a long time! She felt as if someone had ripped apart the dark curtain that had hung before her eyes for the past 30 years.

She fed Krishnalal affectionately, and when the time came for him to leave, she said, 'I have something to tell you—you can always come here for your meals, if you don't mind the food. How can you last at your old age if you go starving? You don't have to pay me anything in return. The Sonarbene Thakur family are on the lookout for a maid. I can work there morning and evening. I'll join work tomorrow—will you come? It is no good asking you, is there? Don't I know you!'

Krishnalal laughed. 'A good idea—let me eat out of your hands for now. I have been wanting to for a long time—but I have to go. I will try to get back late in the evening—'

A month passed by but Krishnalal didn't reappear. He had showered Golapi with so many gifts in those good old days; he was not one who would sit and sponge off her now that he was in a bad way, especially when Golapi, herself, had aged and there was nothing left for her but to work as a maid.

Krishnalal had missed paying rent for his place in the boarding house for two months. The secretary appeared and asked, 'What about the rent, Krishnalal babu?'

'You can see I've lost my job, Khetra babu, I don't have a penny—in the situation how can I…'

'But you must also consider how it would be possible for me to make up, out of my own pocket, for your non-payment every month. Take a couple of days to think about it—then vacate the place so that I can make an alternative arrangement.'

Krishnalal found himself in a fix. He had no money to feed himself with, now he was about to lose the roof over his head. He managed to pass the next three days, slaking his hunger with dal and rice from the cut-price hotel, with money borrowed from a couple of former friends. Then starvation stared at his face. At times he made do with a few paise worth of *chhatu* or *muri*—just *chhatu* without any molasses to go with it. He filled his stomach with water—pure, fresh tap water.

The manager of the mess turned up again.

'Have you arranged something?'

'Today? Actually I had thought…'

'Tomorrow is the first day of the month. I have a person ready to take your place. He has paid me two month's rent in advance and will pay again this month. I've family responsibilities, Sir—how can I cope with a loss of income. Take your things and leave at once—I can forgo the money you owe me.'

Krishnalal was out on the street with all his belongings—a tin trunk and a filthy bedding—early that morning. It was the monsoon season and it was hard for him to find a storage space.

Golapi had enquired after him twice at the mess, had sat on the pavement waiting for him. The mess manager would not have allowed an ill-reputed woman like her to step into the building. Krishnalal slinked away, seeing her from afar. He knew he couldn't land up at her place. She would have raised the roof, weeping and wailing, and prevented him from leaving.

Krishnalal was acquainted with the owner of a tea stall the on the big street some distance from the mess. He begged to be allowed to keep his luggage temporarily at his place and roamed the neighborhood without a thought. All of a sudden lie found himself in Ahirtola quay on the banks of the Ganges.

Krishnalal hadn't eaten since the morning. Buying a penny worth of corn of the cob from a Hindustani corn-seller, he sat feasting happily by the riverside. It would have been so nice if he could smoke a bidi now, he thought. A young fellow, bag in hand, came and sat on the cement-bound platform, spreading a duster. The fellow dug his hand into his pocket as he was about to sit. He looked around. Noticing Krishnalal, he asked, 'Could you please see to my bag, 1 would like to go and buy a paisa worth of bidis.' The fellow gave Krishnalal a bidi when he got back. Somehow Krishnalal had guessed the person was one of the many travelling salesmen. 'Do you hawk goods?' he asked.

'Yes, Sir.'

'What do you sell?'

'Surgical ointment—for wounds.'

'Do you make enough? How much commission do you get?'

'Quite substantial—the only thing is that 1 have to carry a knife along with me to cut and demonstrate—that's the problem!' The fellow rolled up his sleeve. His arm had deep gashes made by a knife from his shoulder down to his wrist.

Krishnalal shuddered. 'What's this? Don't you feel the pain?

The fellow laughed. 'Of course I do—but the wounds heal after an application of the ointment.'

'How much do you earn?'

'Anything between 24 to 35 rupees a month.' A pall of gloom fell on Krishnalal's face. 35 rupees after all the hard work! Time was when he earned upto 60 or 70 rupees a month, trading in Dattapukur's oil for rheumatism. He never had to make gashes on his arm for that. There was nothing attractive about being a salesman anymore; he wouldn't opt for it now.

The next day Krishnalal left Calcutta for his village. He reached his house in Ilshekhali, walking seven kilometers after getting off the train at Basirhat. He had no one in the village save some distant relatives. His ancestral homestead was overgrown with weeds. How long could a simple thatched hut hold out when Krishnalal had neither visited the place nor taken care of it. Krishnalal was home for the last time, 18 years ago, to attend the funeral of an aunt. He had stayed a few days then; he had come there again now.

His relatives offered him a place to stay. Nevertheless, within a few days, Krishnalal began to feel stifled. He had no appetite for country life, no experience of living in a village for any length of time. People there didn't know how to talk, were hardly friendly and didn't drink tea. Even the beggars in the streets of Calcutta knew about tea! Above everything, the village was full of swamps and wild woods. Krishnalal couldn't sleep at nights because of mosquitoes. Every household was afflicted with malaria.

Krishnalal didn't feel like staying on, though lord knew he tried. He was horrified to find the village folk in a nodding-off state all day long! They would gather under the shade of a tree in the Charaktala grounds, hubble-bubble in hand, and confabulate with others, morning till evening. They hardly did any work and yet dropped off to sleep the moment their stomachs were filled. Their afternoon nap always stretched till four in the evening—then some would get up and proceed red-eyed to the market for a few purchases. Gossip would continue there, as well, with men visiting shops and sitting down to smoke. And so their time in the market would stretch for three long hours—till they returned home, late in the evening, to eat and sleep. Kerosene had become dear. No one liked to keep the lamp burning at night. So what was left? More home visits, sitting in the dark for a little chit-chat, pulling at the hubble-bubble and then crawling into bed. Thus, their day was done. What kind of a life was it anyway? Krishnalal was certainly not used to it. Yet people there never stopped complaining, 'Dada we can hardly make do, we are in such a miserable condition!' But where was the effort to lessen the misery? Krishnalal had spent 30 years of his life in hard work in Calcutta. He could hardly tolerate this kind of indolence.

What had been Krishnalal's kind of life? He had to finish his bath under the tap, in the floor below, the minute he was up, otherwise, with the place getting crowded with people, he would have missed his turn. So many came—persons from the goldsmith shop, the shawl vendor, tailors and porters, everyone collected there to gather water or to wash the rice. Men and woman stood in rows, carrying pitchers, the servants of the third floor mess—everybody hard at work, bound to the city clock. 'O, it's late—nearly 6 o'clock, where's the time for work!' The day would commence and with the clock barely striking eight, the babus would arrive and demand rice—not brooking a minute's delay!

Krishnalal would arrive at the Sealdah station, bag in hand, the moment he would finish his bath. He would be at Barasat at 7:10 am, Naihati at 7:25, board the Ranaghat passenger train at 7:45, Bongaon Local at 8:30, Dattapukur at 8:50 and the Kesto Nagar Local at 9:10...and begin his day's work thus— 'Oil for rheumatism, oil from Dattapukur... All kinds of arthitis, inflammation, pain, headaches, stomach ache all—will disappear with an application of only this...this oil...Gentlemen, the medicine has acquired such reputation among people taking this journey for the last 30 years...' He would go on and on till 12 noon. His morning's work would come to an end only when the train left Shantipur at 12:55. What a life! What happiness! What a lot of money he earned each day. Cash would come rolling in, get blown by the evening. Those who knew how to make money knew how to spend it!

Krishnalal managed to stay on in the village for another month—after that he gave that up as a bad job. An idle life was intolerable for him. He had never, ever, lived folding up his knees like a tortoise. He felt he would either go mad or die if he continued that way. But then how was he to feed himself in Calcutta? He couldn't think of any solution. He knew that the Indian Drug Syndicate would never take him back, although he could try—beg Mr Bose one more time...And if nothing came of it then there was always the young salesman of Ahirtala quay he could go to. But how could he, in his old age, submit himself to making gashes on his arm? There was no job in the world to compare with the job of a salesman. Such honor and such comfort! But was it honorable to inflict deep wounds on one's arm in order to demonstrate the virtue of a medicine? The problem was Krishnalal wasn't fit for life in the village. He was used to work, not to an insensate existence in the country. He couldn't live on air!

Some people advised him to plough the couple of bighas of land he owned in the coming winter, while others said, 'There's a piece of land next to the shallow pond. It's your ancestral property, Kestokhuro; plant some *mankachu* there in the winter months. You can bring in money selling them in the market. Sow seeds during the winter…' Krishnalal felt like laughing. How would the fools know that even if he were to sell a year's yield of *kachu* crop and pumpkins, his earnings would never match what he collected, working in Calcutta each month. He had *that* kind of a job! Eventually, however, Krishnalal packed his belongings and returned to the city. He decided if had to live he would live in style.

He met many old travelling salesmen in the train—those working for Nabashakti Oushadhalaya, Kaviraj Anagamohan Deb, Biswas and Co., Indian Drug Syndicate and others. They all knew him and treated him with respect.

'My goodness Kesto da, you're here, we don't see you these days!'

'From where have you landed, Kesto? Did you go and get married—at your age?'

'Which company do you work for now, Kesto da? We don't see you on the train anymore!'

'Were you attending to your ancestral property? And why wouldn't you brother, since you own land…We have nothing to fall back on. Biswas and Co. will make us work till the last drop of our blood. I feel so envious when I think of you! You have landed property worth 200 rupees a year, did you say? Astounding! Then you are a…' etc., etc.,

A person offered him a bidi, another held out an open betel leaf box. They were his old chums. How could he have spent so many days in the 'sleeping castle' of the village, leaving them behind? There would be a job for him here—money, all kinds of pleasure, and of course *intimate* friends. He wouldn't ever leave Calcutta again—he would die here if he had to.

Krishnalal hunted for a job for the next 15 or 20 days but couldn't find one. Mr Bose categorically refused to even consider him. Nowadays the canvassers were young, good-looking men. They wore long whiskers, had sandals wrapped around their feet and the voice of the stage Ram. They were the ones in demand—not old fogies like him. 'When one is old—I mean there's no vacancy now, will write to you when there is one—' was the kind of response he got.

Krishnalal put up at his old mess but slept in the veranda now. He hadn't gone to see Golapi—he was not yet ready to see her. He starved for two whole days, then took himself to the Ahirtala quay in the hope of meeting the young seller of oil, with gashes on his arm. The boy had told him he arrived there on the steamer from Bali everyday at 12:30. Krishnalal looked for him for over a week but couldn't trace him. His misery reached its ultimate depth. He knew he couldn't go on—was he also losing his expertise in selling medicine? He hadn't worked for so long! He hadn't held forth for months—his voice had fallen into disuse; he feared some stripling of a salesman might beat him at the game.

That day Krishnalal went over to the Dalhousie square corner, taking along his little box. He started giving his canvassing speech, throwing his arms about. He had to practice his art, besides wanting to test his skills. He had to see if he could still draw crowds of buyers. He wanted to prove to himself his voice could compete with that of the boy who played Ram on the stage. 'See, this is the oil from Dattapukur, for all kinds of arthritic pains, headaches, toothaches, arm pain, shoulder pain—dear gentleman it is this very medicine that I have been selling in the Laldighi corner for the last 30 years…' He looked around him after five or six minutes of speaking and found quite a crowd had gathered around him. One person pushed forward and said 'Can you give me a small bottle?'

Krishnalal replied with a solemn voice. 'I don't carry medicines with me. I work for the publicity department of the Indian Drug Syndicate. Those who need the medicine must go to 106C Haridhan Poddar Lane, to the office of the Indian Drug Syndicate, with a slip from me. You'll get 4 per cent commission. Stay, let me give you the slip.'

Six days passed this way, Krishnalal became addicted to the game.

He would go to Dalhousie corner, carrying his box, every afternoon at three and begin his speech. People would throng to him. One day, as he was relating the virtues of Dattapukur oil a person barged in and stood in front of him.

Krishnalal was struck with amazement. It was Nrityagopal Bose of the Indian Drug Syndicate himself!

Bose looked at Krishnalal straight in the eyes, 'Here—come this side.'

Krishnalal left the crowd of people and stood shamefaced in front of his old boss.

'What's all this?' Bose asked.

Krishnalal scratched his head and looked sheepish. 'Sir, I am keeping up with the practice or else...'

'My word! I was wondering what was going on. A hundred or more people had been coming to my place with slips of paper from you for the last few days—I was taken aback by the phenomenon. I haven't sold so much in a long time! Besides, this is the dull season. Everyone who came said they had come hearing about us from our publicity officer at the Laldighi comer. I said to myself—'I must go and see what it is all about.' And I must say I am rather pleased about the effort you have put in...'

'Sir, I thought let me try—although I don't have the voice of the stage Ram that all your new salesmen seem to possess—'

'Listen to me, Come to my office today itself. I am appointing you the Head Canvasser. You'll get 60 rupees pay plus commission. You will have to supervise the work of the youngsters—train them in their jobs, see that they work properly—understand? Come, come along with me straightway in my car.'

Golapi was blowing into a makeshift oven, made out of a pail, in the narrow platform of her unfastened room in Nabin Kundu Lane. It was late in the evening—a familiar voice called out to her. 'Golapi, dear, come out and take hold of the things…my arms are about to fall off.'

The original Bengali story was first published in *Nabagoto*. January 1946.

ACKNOWLEDGEMENTS

The translator wishes to acknowledge the support and help of Bibhutibhushan Bandyopadhaya's son, Late Taradas Bandyopadhaya and his grandson, Tathagata Banerjee, who have made this volume possible. The translation of these stories could not have been accomplished without their active encouragement. I would also like to thank Rusati Sen for her valuable comments, and Anita Agnihotri for re-introducing me to the works of Bibhutibhushan and for allowing me to share her enthusiasm and excitement.

Translating Bibhutibhushan has been an awesome task, and while I mourn the loss of the lucidity and grace of the writer's original Bengali in my English rendering, I sincerely hope I have been able to do my best to preserve the tone and force of his writings.